HE GOT ME IN MY FEELINGS

BY: KELLZ KIMBERLY

Acknowledgements

I'm never really good at this type of thing so let me see if I can get this out quick and easy without any tears. I just honestly want to say thank you to all my readers and supporters. Y'all just don't know how much love I have for y'all. The reason I keep going with my writing is because of y'all. To every reader that has ever one clicked any of my books, left a review, shared a link I just want to say thank you from the bottom of my heart thank you.

Jamal you are my everything and what's understood doesn't have to be explained. Five years and counting, at the end of the day it will always be me and you.

I have to give a special shout out to Tiece. You are the real MVP for real, for real! You took a chance on me and I told you I got you, and I still do. I want to say thank you for everything you have done for me and continue to do. We may not see eye to eye on certain things, but you always show me you have my best interest at heart, and that means a lot. You are the true definition of a publisher. You have helped me in so many ways that it's crazy. It's not about the money with you and that's what I love. You genuinely want to see people succeed in this business. I have nothing but love for you and I will always have you for whatever.

Ebony my light skin, the relationship that we have built in the past year is one that I am grateful for. Our friendship goes beyond the literary world. You are honestly one of the most genuine people I have ever met and I just want to say thank you for just simple being there for me.

3

To everyone at Tiece Mickens Presents, y'all already know how we get down. The support we show each other is real and I'm glad to be signed with each and everyone of you.

Niqua, the friendship that we have built in the last couple months is amazing. Whenever I write anything, you are one of the people I think to send it to first. I thank you for helping me and just reading everything I send you. Our friendship goes beyond the writing world and just know, we are turning up in Atlanta.

Victoria, you have been rocking with me since day one. I don't consider you a reader, I consider you a friend. You are always there to help when I get stuck or when I need you to read something. Plus, you are the voice of reason when I'm ready to do something crazy with these characters. You are another one of my favorite test readers because you tell me like it is instead of just saying you like it, and I appreciate that.

Rikida, you have been the biggest help when it came to this book. I don't know how many times I sent you this book so you could test read it for me, but every time I did send it, you gave great feedback. I don't think you know it, but you really pushed me with this book. Every time you gave me feedback, you were excited about the book, which pushed me to make the next chapters even better. Overall, I just want to say thank you.

Por'schea, girl, we clicked as soon as we started talking. I don't even view you as one of my readers, you're my friend. You are always there when I need you and I love that you are taking a chance on me. I got nothing but love for you and there is nothing else to do but go up from here.

To the ladies of Kellz K Publishing, I have to give y'all a shout out because it's because of y'all that I am able to check off a goal off my list. Without y'all I wouldn't be a publisher. We about to take this literary game by storm. #Summer16 is ours!!!!

To everyone in my group, BRP Presents: Bring Your Own Tea, thank you for rocking with me because y'all go hard for y'all girl. Its amazing how one group can bring so many women together who support and build each other up. I don't care what no one says my group is the shit.

To everyone that has helped me promote my book, read any of my books and given me feedback, I want to say thank you so much because it means a lot.

To all my readers that have Facebook, if y'all want to keep up with my new releases, sneak peeks and giveaways, join my Facebook group, BRP Presents: Bring Your Own Tea.

To get in contact with me, feel free to email me or hit me up on social media. Feel free to hit me up with questions and feedback.

Facebook: Kellz Kimberly

Facebook Group: BRP Presents: Bring Your Own Tea

Twitter: _KellzK

Instagram: __Lacedupchic

Snap Chat: kellzkayy

Email: Kellz@TMPresents.com

Kellz K. Publishing is now accepting Submissions in the Following Genres....

***African American Romance

***Urban Fiction

***Multicultural Romance

***Street Lit

Please submit the first 3 chapters of your work, along with a Brief Description of your story line to: kellz@tmpresents.com

Chapter 1: Royce

"Here at the Cracked Mug, we like to give new talent a try and tonight, we have someone who is very new. Welcome to the stage, Royce Silva!"

I heard my name being called to the stage, but there was no claps or cheers. I walked on feeling as though the grilled chicken salad I had for lunch would repay me a visit at any moment. I walked up to the mic, eager to let my voice be heard, but nervous at the same time.

"Hey, I'm Royce," I said just above a whisper. I wiped my sweaty palms on the black skinny jeans I wore.

"Just get on with it!" someone yelled.

"Yeah!" another person yelled.

I closed my eyes and counted to three before I opened my mouth to sing. No words came out. I was on the verge of tears as the people in the crowd booed me off the stage. I wanted to run away and hide underneath a blanket I didn't have. The more I tried to sing, the more the crowd roared. My heart was beating a mile a minute. I took the first step that would lead me from in front of the angry crowd.

No Royce, you have to do this, I thought to myself, trying to build up my confidence. I gripped the mic for dear life.

"It could all be so simple, but you'd rather make it hard. Loving you is like a battle and we both end up with scars. Tell me, who I have to be, to get some reciprocity? No one loves you more than me and no one ever will." The band behind me started to join in as I really began to sing.

"Is this just a silly game that forces you to act this way? Forces you to scream my name, then pretend that you can't stay. Tell me, who I have to be, to get some reciprocity? No one loves you more than me and no one ever will. No matter how I think we grow, you always seem to let me know, it ain't workin'. It ain't workin'. And when I try to walk away, you'd hurt yourself to make me stay; this is crazy. This crazy."

As I began to really get into the song, I found my confidence. There were people in the crowd yelling for me to sing that song. I was pouring my all into this song and singing my heart out because this was my truth. My truth.

"I keep letting you back in. How can I explain myself? As painful as this thing has been, I just can't be with no one else. See, I know what we got to do. You let go and I'll let go too. 'Cause no one's hurt me more than you and no one ever will. Care for me, care for me. I know you care for me. There for me, there for me. Said you'd be there for me. Cry for me, cry for me. You said you'd die for me. Give to me, give to me. Why won't you live for me?"

Once again, I was on the verge of tears, this song cut so deep and, at the moment, I was wearing my emotions on my sleeve.

"Care for me, care for me. I know you care for me. There for me, there for me. Said you'd be there for me. Cry for me, cry for me. You said you'd die for me. Give to me, give to me. Why won't you live for me?" The band was still playing as my voice faded out. I released my grip on the mic, did a little bow, and walked off the stage. The crowd started yelling but, this time, it wasn't negative. The claps and cheers I was looking for before now echoed throughout the room. I went to the back behind stage, grabbed my leather jacket and my duffle bags, and headed out of the back door.

It was a cool April night; the slight breeze hit my face as I walked down Queens Blvd. I hit the corner and waved down a cab. Getting in, I gave the cabbie the address and leaned my head back, getting comfortable. I know y'all wondering why I got up there singing one of the saddest songs ever written. The song was my truth; I'm in a relationship that I try to walk away from but every time I start to walk away, he pulls me back in. It was a never ending cycle between Addison and I. He wanted to fuck up and I was just supposed to take it. I saw the potential in him, which was the reason I continued to allow him back in. Potential was starting to not be enough. I was tired of the empty promises and the lies he fed me on the regular. It was always baby, I love you and you know you're my world and in a blink of an eye, it turned into you're the reason I cheat. I was to blame, even when he was doing wrong. I accepted the blame every time, just to have him sleep in my bed every night. I accepted the blame because the love I had for him allowed me to.

Addison and I were the typical high school sweethearts. I was a freshman; he was a junior. Lust at first sight and love at first touch. He approached me and I thought I was the shit. One of the most popular guys in school wanted my name and number; of course, I gave it to him. His boyish good looks and pretty smile should have come with a warning label. 'Heartbreak and hard dick is the only thing I'm offering'; I assumed the label would read. All through high school, I was hit with the rumors of Addison cheating on me. I was young, dumb, and full of cum, so no one could tell me anything.

Fast forwards six years later; I was a junior at LIU while Addison was a party promoter throwing and hosting parties at his father's club. Being at the club every other night presented Addison with numerous opportunities to cheat. Like the dog he was, he took just about everyone and yet, my ass still stayed. I know y'all probably calling me dumb and weak, but I wasn't neither. Like the song says, when I try to walk away, you'd hurt yourself to make me stay. I was tired of the vicious cycle we called our relationship. The six years we had been together had been filled with more hurt than love, more bad than good. However, today was the day I walked away from it all. Today was the day I washed my hands clean of the situation. A slight chuckle escaped my lips as I thought about how I caught Addison cheating on me in the apartment that we shared just seven hours ago.

"Baby, where are you?" I called out, looking for Addison.

He was supposed to pick me up from school to take me to my doctor's appointment. I ran out of birth control and needed to get a refill. Addison never showed, so I had to ask my mother to pick me up and drop me off. I caught the train back home because my mother wasn't going to travel to Queens to drop me off. I honestly was getting tired of the neglect Addison showed me. It just seemed that, after six years of dating, I still wasn't a priority to him. He wasn't running the streets like must dudes, but he was always in the club, which was just as bad.

I went towards the kitchen to grab a bottle of water since Addison never answered me when I called out to him. After finishing my water, I headed for our bedroom to take a quick nap before I went to the Cracked Mug. The Cracked Mug was a whole in the wall coffee shop a couple of blocks from here. I liked to go there and listen to the artists sing. I always wanted to go up there and sing, but my shyness always got the best of me.

The door was slightly opened; I figured Addison was in there sleep. I pushed the door open, but it was dark in the room. I flicked the light on and gasped at what I saw. Addison was in bed sleeping while some chick was lying against his back. I wanted to scream out in agony, but I covered my mouth before anything could come out. I turned the light off before it woke anyone up, closed the door back, and slid down the wall. My heart was literally broken; it felt as though it hit the bottom of my stomach. This wasn't the first time Addison cheated on me, but to see it with my own eyes was another thing. The pain I was experiencing was a pain I never felt before. I sat against the wall crying, trying to get my thoughts together. I could have gone in there showing my ass but that wouldn't do anything because I've done that before. Then, on the other hand, I could've walked away but, at the same time, I would feel like less than a woman because I allowed Addison to do me dirty.

As if on cue, Mary J Blige's song Not Gon' Cry started playing from my phone. I pulled it from my back pocket while singing along. I got up from off the floor, dusted my pants off, wiped my eyes, and went into his hallway closet where he kept all his sneakers. Addison was a sneaker head foreal. He had everything from Jordans to the red Octobers. Not to mention, the foreign sneakers and shoes he had. I took out box after box, dumping them into the bath tub. Once I got every pair in there, I pulled out a bottle of bleach and poured it on them, along with some ammonia. I would've set that bitch on fire, but I wasn't ready to go to jail on a double murder charge. I grabbed a couple of my duffle bags, filling them with as much shoes and clothes as I could. I left the key to the apartment we once shared on the coffee table and walked out, never looking back.

"We're here miss," the cabbie said.

I looked at the meter and paid the cabbie my fare. I walked up the couple of stairs to my mother's apartment and used my key to let myself in. Closing the door behind me, I walked further into the house but didn't see anyone. I was thankful because I wasn't ready to answer any questions I knew my mother would have. I lugged all of my bags into my old room and dropped them on the floor. I crawled into bed crying myself to sleep, but this was going to be the last time I shed a tear over Addison Mitchell.

∞"Royce, wake up now and get that boy away from my door!"

"Okay, okay mom," I grumbled.

I slowly got out of bed, slipped my feet into my slippers, and followed my mom to the front door.

"You don't have to stand by; I can handle this," I told her.

"Like hell I don't. Just handle your business, so I can go to sleep. I'm just getting in and I have to go right back later this afternoon." My mother worked as a security guard overnight at a parking garage.

"Addison, what could you possibly want?" I asked, swinging the door open.

"Royce, don't try to act like you didn't fuck up all my sneakers. Not to mention the smell of bleach and ammonia could've killed me. What the fuck is wrong with you!" he yelled.

"No, the question is what's the matter with you? I come home to find you in bed, not even in bed, in our bed with another woman."

My mother gasped as Addison had a look of shock on his face. He went to start talking and I just started shaking my head.

"I no longer want to hear the excuses you have. I can't keep allowing you to walk all over me as if I'm a doormat. I am diminishing myself as a woman by allowing you to remain in my life. You don't have to worry about anything because I don't have ill feelings towards you. I'm not mad at you and I don't blame you. I blame myself. This last incident that happened is my fault because I should have left you alone before, so this one right here I'm taking the blame for. With that being said, I wish you nothing but the best; this is good bye." I closed the door in his face and went to go back in my bed room to go back to sleep, but my mother stopped me.

"Oh, no hunny; you are not walking away without explaining this shit to me."

"Mom, there is nothing to explain. I went home and caught him in bed with another woman. That was the final straw for me and I'm walking away," I sighed.

"You should have been walked away. You invested six years into his cheating ass and you can't get those six years back."

"I know mom."

"Don't 'I know mom' me. I have been telling you that nothing good can come from being with that man. I can't help that I want the best for my daughter and he wasn't it."

"I hear you talking Nijah." I laughed.

"I hope you do hear me talking. Never allow a man to get so comfortable with you that he no longer cares about your feelings. The same way a man works to get you should be the same way he continues to work to keep you."

I wasn't about to sit here and listen to my mother preach on because I didn't need the lecture. "Mom, I'm serious; I hear everything that you are saying."

"I don't think you do. I'm trying to make sure you listen to the lessons I'm teaching you because I didn't listen to my mother when she was trying to teach me. I've told you the stories of my wild days and you're the result of one of those wild stories. My mother tried to teach me about men and I didn't want to listen. I allowed your father to walk all over me, all because he came home to me at night and I assumed it was love. It took him leaving me right before you were born for me to realize that I was worth more. It's strange but, in that moment, I can honestly say I figured out my worth."

"I may not act like it, but I appreciate all the advice that you give me, mom; I really do."

"Well, just promise me that you will take this piece of advice with you in your dating journey."

"I promise."

"All I'm trying to do is teach you the difference between a man who flatters you and a man who compliments you. A man who spends money on you and a man who invests in you. A man who views you as property and a man who views you properly. A man who lusts after you and a man who loves you. Royce, find a man who compliments you, who views you properly and a man who loves you; once you find a man who does that, you will find a man who knows women are God's gift to man and will be able to teach your son the same." My mother got up, kissed me on the cheek, then went towards her bedroom.

I went into my room as my mother's words lingered in my head. She was absolutely right; I needed to find a man that truly knew the worth and depth of a woman.

Chapter 2: Karma

"Camellia, make sure that everything is ready for tonight. I don't want no fuck ups with this."

"I got you, Karma; you didn't put me in charge for nothing." She winked while walking past, sliding something into my hand. I stuck my hand in my pocket because from the material, I already knew what it was.

Camellia was a certified freak and I could appreciate that, but there was a time and place for everything and now wasn't the time. When it came to business, Camellia was in charge of all my baggers and cookers. She would make sure everything was good, then bring it to my spot over in Mount Haven. Outside of business, she was my stress reliever and I was hers. I was told to never mix business with pleasure, but Camellia was the expectation. We both understood our roles in each other's lives, which made everything a whole lot smoother.

You see, I was on a mission and the mission didn't involve a girlfriend. My mission was strictly about that money, that bread, that chicken, that gaup. In other words, money was the motive for a young nigga like me. I know y'all probably tired of the same old story and shit but, hey, what you want me to say. When you grow up in the hood without a mother, father, or any parental guidance, you go out there and get it by any means necessary. I grew up in the boogie down, going from group homes to park benches. My life was rough. While some dudes were out here going nights without anything to eat, I was out here going without food for weeks. Yeah, I could have stayed at the group homes the state put me in, but who wants to be on a schedule? They managed your time as if it was a nine to five. I didn't have time for that because they weren't helping me get what I need.

If it wasn't for Red, I don't know where a nigga would be. The way we met was fucking crazy, but it honestly changed my life forever.

After leaving the fifth group home I was placed in this year, I went straight to Van Cortlandt Park. It was around twelve in the morning and I was just trying to catch a couple of z's before it was time for me to figure out what the hell I was going to do with myself. I was only fifteen and didn't have no one in this world to have my back. I was in this cold world alone, but I was destined to come out on top by any means. I was half-sleep and half-awake when I felt the cold steel tap against my shoulder.

"Ayo lil nigga, I need you to get the fuck up off this bench and make a move."

"I can't do that," I said, never acknowledging the dude who was talking.

"Ayo nigga, do you know who you talking to? When my man says get the fuck off the bench, you get the fuck off the bench." I sat up on the bench and ran my hands over face. Looking at me, you wouldn't think I was fifteen, I stood at about 6'4" and had as much facial hair as any grown man.

"I don't care who the fuck said what. I'm not getting off this bench," I told them. Yeah, I may have been young and these niggas had guns, but I wasn't nobody's punk bitch.

"I know you see these guns in our hands, so you must be ready to die." The one that was doing all the talking couldn't have been the nigga in charge. When someone was in charge, they talked less and acted more. This nigga talking was doing the most.

"Just like I see those guns in your hand, I know you see me sleeping on this bench. You killing me ain't doing shit but putting me out this misery I call life."

"Don't nobody give a fuck about yo sad fucking story, just get the fuck up." He went to grab me by the collar of my shirt and just as he did, I slipped a blade from out my mouth and swiftly slid it across his arm.

"Ahhh Fuck!" dude screamed while backing up. He looked at me with fire in his eyes while I looked at him, letting him know I was ready for whatever.

"The fuck you doing carrying blades around in your mouth? That's some straight up bitch shit. The fuck you got a pussy in the sweats or some shit," the dude gritted.

I side eyed the other dude as he just stood there. *"Nigga, carrying a blade is only bitch shit when a bitch do it. I got nine inches you can suck if you into that type of shit. But don't ever get it confused; ain't nothing bitch about me."* I grabbed my imprint through my sweats, letting him know I was serious. I was talking *mad shit to this nigga who could end my life with a single bullet but, at this point, I didn't have shit to lose. The way I saw it, death probably would've been easier for me then life.*

"Say your hail Mary's nigga because I don't play that disrespectful shit." He cocked his gun and I stood there with my chest poked out, ready for my fate.

"Chill the fuck out Max and go get your fucking hand checked out and shit."

"Red, the fuck you talking 'bout chill the fuck out. This nigga gonna tell me to suck his dick like I'm some bitch made nigga. I don't know about you but the way I see it, that shit is a straight death sentence."

"Yo Max, you know I don't repeat myself twice. Go check your fucking hand out," the dude that was quiet the whole time ordered. The dude who was popping shit glared at me, then walked off mumbling some shit.

"What's yo name youngin'?" dude asked me.

"Karma," I told him.

"Karma huh?" he chuckled. "Come take a ride with me. The way you just handled yo self is impressive."

"Thanks, but I don't know you like that to be taking rides. Yo mans wants to off me so that shit isn't even a smart move."

"You see that shit right there. That's the type of shit I need on my team. You a thinker and fear isn't shit to you but a word.

Those two things are a deadly combination. If you won't take this ride with me, then take this walk."

"Yo, Karma, we got to go. Smitty just hit me and said he need some extra shit," Trench said, pulling me out of my thoughts.

"Ight, we out," I told him. We hopped into my white on white 2014 Mercedes Benz and took off towards Mott Haven projects, where we had about three traps.

"Man, I can't wait until this whole trap shit is over. A nigga is ready for bigger and better things," Trench vented.

"Patience is virtue my nigga," I told him. I met Trench when Red put me on. We were hustling the same block together night and day. I respected him off the strength that the nigga never left the block. He was a get money dude like myself and that shit was straight love.

"Nigga, you been telling me that shit since we been hugging the block. A nigga is over that shit, on the real."

"Look, just be grateful for how Red put us on. We started hugging the block at the age of fifteen, then got upgraded to the traps at seventeen. Nigga, we twenty now and we run all of Mott Haven. We making more money then a little bit. Our hustle speaks for itself and when Red feels it's right to put us higher on the food chain, then he will do so. For now, just worry about getting this paper."

"You right my nigga," Trench agreed.

"I know I am. I'm the smart one out the bunch," I joked.

"Yeah, ight my nigga. On another note, we rolling to that party they havin' at Ladiez in Kickz later tonight?"

"As long as everything is straight with Smitty, we can ride out."

"Ight, my nigga," Trench said, nodding his head as I turned the radio up.

50 cent's song *Hustler's Ambition* blared through the speakers. I bobbed my head to the beat, rocking to the song. When the first verse came up, I couldn't help but to rap along.

"America's got a thing for this gangsta's shit, they love me. Black chucks, black skullies, leather Pelle-Pelle. I take spit over raymo shit, I'm a vandal. Got that silver duct tape on my Trey Eight Handle. The woman on my life bring confusion shit. So like Nino from New Jack, I'll have to cancel that bitch. Look at me, this is the life I chose. Niggas around me so cold, man my heart done froze up. I build an empire on the low, the narc's don't know. I'm the weatherman, I take that coco leaf and make that snow. Sit back, watch it turn to dope, watch it go out the door. O after O, you know, homey I'm just triple beam, dreaming. Niggas be scheming, I'm fiendin' to live a good life. The fiends just fiendin'. Conceal my weapon nice and easy, so you can't see. The penitentiary is definitely out the question for me. I want the finer things in my life, so I hustle. Nigga, you get in my way when I'm trying to get mine and I'll buck you. I don't care who you run with, or where you from, nigga fuck you. I want to fine the thing that's in my life so I hustle."

That first verse in the song was exactly how I was feeling. I wanted the finer things in life, so I hustled. Once I got to where I needed to be, then the woman would come later but, for now, dead presidents was the only thing I was stackin' and countin.'

Chapter 3: Royce

I I I I I I I I ride for my bitches. I'm so fuckin' rich, I cop rides for my bitches. Dollar menu fries, apple pies, out the bitches. I drop a freestyle and get a rise outta bitches; bitches, my bitches. I need a nigga with some diff'rent strokes, Todd Bridges. Shout out to my main bitches and my side bitches. Need a nigga with some good neck, ostriches....my nigga.

My phone ringing off the hook woke me up from my peaceful sleep. After that conversation with my mother, I wanted nothing more than to go back to sleep and wish the last six years with Addison didn't happen. Reaching over to my nightstand, I found my phone.

"Where you at Royce?" Callie asked as soon as I answered.

"In my bed, sleep." I yawned.

"Get up; you said you would go with me to the Ladiez in Kickz party."

"Callie, that's Addison's party and I'm not trying to see him nor be around him. I ended things with him this morning."

"Girl, it's about time; now, we have to go out and celebrate. What better way to celebrate other than showing up at his event and showing the fuck out," she said, hype as hell.

"I honestly just want to sleep Callie. I'm tired as hell."

"I don't want to hear that. Where are you, your mother's house?"

"Yes, where else would I be?"

"No need for the smart remarks missy. I'll be there in like an hour. Make sure you washed your ass by the time I get there. I'll bring you something to wear."

"Whatever Callie."

"I love you too." She giggled, hanging up the phone.

I let out a slight scream of frustration before placing my phone back on the nightstand. Callie was my girl but, sometimes, she took things above and beyond. I met her my freshman year of college; we only been friends for three years, but she was always there for me when it came to Addison. She was crazy as hell but always supportive, even if it wasn't in the ways I would like her to be.

"Royce, are you up?" my mother asked while lightly knocking on the door.

"Yeah, come in," I told her.

"I hope you're not staying in the bed all day. You're only twenty-one baby; go out and have some fun. For the past six years, Addison has been the only person you have known. Meet new people and mingle," my mother explained, sitting on my bed.

"You sound like Callie, you know that." I laughed.

"Then Callie is a smart woman. There is no point in dwelling over a man that did more bad than good. Now, get up and go have some fun or something."

"I'm actually going to party with Callie."

"Good, just make sure you're home before I get home tonight and if you're staying out, just send me a text or something. I love you and will see you in the morning."

"Love you and have a good day at work." I leaned over and gave my mother a hug.

She walked out the door and I got up to go take a shower. My mother was right. I didn't need to be sitting around moping over Addison because it was his lost, not mine. Just like that, the foul mood I was in earlier was gone. I was gonna put my break up with Addison behind me, so I could party the night away.

∞ ∞ ∞

"Royce, come on before we're late for the party!" Callie said, knocking on the bathroom door.

"Callie, when are we not late to a party? Stop actin' like you don't know wassup." I laughed, opening the bathroom door.

"It's better to arrive late than to arrive ugly." She giggled, slapping me on the ass.

"Exactly. Now let's go in your room, so we can check out our outfits."

We stood in my wall length mirror, making sure that both of our outfits were on point. I was kind of nervous about the outfit Callie picked out for me but after putting it on, I looked good as fuck.

"Royce, whose man you trying to steal?" Callie smiled, looking at my reflection in the mirror.

I was rocking these black spandex pants that had suspenders attached. I paired it with a black tight-fitting muscle shirt and a pair of thigh high boots. My outfit was similar to the one Ciara wore in the video Promise.

"Everyone! Just call me Ms. Steal Yo Nigga." I winked at her, then giggled a little. I was lying my ass off because I wasn't about that stealing someone's man life. I done had my man stolen for a night, so I know how it feels.

"You know damn well you lying, but I like the enthusiasm," Callie said, going over to my bed and sitting down.

"I should've went to school for fashion instead of business because I picked the hell out of our outfits. I look cute as hell."

She wasn't lying; her outfit was real cute. Callie rocked a cute pair of black acid wash jeans with a white half shirt that was tied in the back. On her feet, she wore a cute pair of black ankle boots with her shoulder length hair parted to where she would have a deep side part, giving her that young Aaliyah feel.

"You're so conceited." I laughed with a roll of my eyes.

"I'm conceited, I got a reason," she sang.

"You play way too much."

"Who said I'm playing? I was so serious."

"Let me finish getting ready because foolin' with you, we will never make it out the door."

I brushed my hair into a ponytail then wrapped a couple of tracks around it, making it longer and fuller. I made sure to part my hair, so I would have that swoop bang in the front. My baby hairs were slicked down to perfection, causing me to smile. One of my favorite features about my face was my dimples. They were deep and showed at the slightest motion of a smile. Giving myself the once over, I made a mental note that I needed to go and get my hair done asap. Other than that, I approved the final outcome of my look and turned towards Callie.

"You a bad bitch." I smiled.

"And ya friend bad too." Callie joined in, standing next to me in the mirror.

"We got that swag, so we drippin' swagu," we sang together.

We giggled then grabbed our things, ready to start our night. I made sure that all the lights were off in the house before locking up and heading outside. Getting in Callie's car, I applied my grape lip gloss, only putting on enough to make my succulent lips pop. As Callie pulled off, I had a feeling this was going to be a night to remember.

Walking into the sneaker store, all eyes were on Callie and I, but this was something we were used to. Whenever we went out, we got stares from people. I never really paid it any mind, but Callie lived for it. She simply loved attention.

"Why these females acting like they got eye problems and shit?" Callie asked, grilling everyone who was grilling us.

"I don't know, but you know it's not even something to worry about."

"I know." She laughed.

I took her hand and pulled her to the dance floor. Dancing was something that we both loved and whenever we touched the floor to dance, we fucked it up. *How Low* by Ludacris was playing when I felt a pair of arms wrap around my body. I did a sexy spin, just to find out who the hands belonged to.

"Royce, why you turnin' around? You know I love when yo ass is pressed against it." Addison smiled.

The sound of his voice alone caused me to catch an instant attitude. "Addison, get your hands off me," I told him, moving out of his grasp.

"Damn Royce, it's like that?" he asked, sounding surprised.

"What part of 'we are over' don't you understand?"

"I don't wanna hear that shit. You and me are a forever thing. We not over until I say we over," he smirked.

"Addison, you are really fucking delusion-"

"Addison, I know you didn't leave me at the bar alone to be in this bitch face," some light bright chick said.

"You don't know me, so please don't call me out my name," I told the girl.

"I don't give a fuck who you are; just stay the fuck out my man's face," she sassed.

I looked at Addison smiling from the corner of my eye. This dude was really standing there like what was going on was entertaining to him.

"Addison, you need to check your chick," I told him.

"No, he needs to stop wasting his time with dog ass bitches," the girl said, right as she shoved me.

I'm not going to lie; the push was unexpected, so I slipped up and almost fell. I regained my composure, then walked back over to her with a devious smile on my face. I wasn't the type to start fights but that didn't mean I wasn't a fighter. I jabbed her quickly in the nose, causing it to gush out blood instantly.

"Damn Royce!" Addison said, rushing to the girl's aid.

I shook my head at him because if he would've intervened, none of this would have happened. Everyone was looking at me and, in this moment, I was ready to go. I looked around and Callie was no longer on the dance floor. I went to go look for her when I felt someone tug at my wrist.

I tried snatching my wrist away, but this dude had the death grip on my hand. I turned towards him and had to look up because dude was as tall as a sky scraper.

"Um, do you mind letting my wrist go?" I asked. I was already in a foul mood because of Addison and his bullshit, so I didn't really need this dude's drama.

24

"I do mind, come here," he said, pulling me closer to him. I didn't know who he was, but I didn't appreciate him wrapping his arms around my waist.

"Butta, why you do that girl like that?" His eyes were low and red.

"You must have me confused with someone else because I don't know who Butta is."

"Don't insult my intelligence Butta. Why you do ole girl like that?" he asked again.

"She felt it was okay to put her hands on me; therefore, giving me the impression it's okay for me to put my hands on her." Not once have I ever felt the need to explain my actions to anyone, which was why I was confused as to why I was explaining myself to him.

"You a feisty one, aren't you?" He laughed.

"Why does it matter?"

"I like that shit in a female." He smiled. His smile was infectious and before I knew it, I was smiling showing off all thirty-two.

"Butta, you got dimples; you must've been cut from my rib." He placed one finger in my dimple as I did the same to him. My dimples were a lot deeper than his, but his were still cute.

"I, uh, need to go," I told him, walking away. The fact that I was so comfortable being hugged up with him worried me. I definitely needed to find Callie and get the hell out of here.

Chapter 4: Karma

Butta was something else; it was like she was straight Henny without any Coke to balance her out. I was off on the side chilling when I saw her punch ole girl in the nose. You know that punch packed some heat behind it to make her nose bleed with one shot. Butta was bad in every aspect of the word. She was a dark chocolate complexion that had me wanting to take a bite out of her plump ass. If I had to take a guess, she was only about 5 feet even but she was thick, just not outrageously thick. Butta was fine as fuck and I almost got caught up in her eyes when I had her pressed against me. Her vibe and aura was mad cool but, as far as I seen it, anything that happened between us wouldn't go as far as the bedroom.

A part of me wanted to pull her back when she walked away, but I wasn't trying to look like no thirsty nigga. Instead of pulling her, I mingled around the joint, talking to a few chicks here and there. About an hour passed and I was ready to go; being out at parties really wasn't my thing. I would rather be getting that bread. I searched the room for Trench and found him over by where the bar was set up. He was taking shots with some chick who was fine as fuck.

"Trench, I'm 'bout to get up out of here."

"Hol' up nigga, it's only one; the night is still young. Callie, this is my nigga, Karma," Trench slurred.

"Nice to meet you." I smiled.

"Nice to meet-"

"Callie, I've been looking for you all over the place for the last hour. I should kick your ass for leaving me hanging to be with some dude." The chick I was trying to help before interrupted.

"Shawty, you rude as fuck; didn't you see us having a conversation?" I questioned. "Not to mention, this place is only but so big."

"Umm, was I talking to you?" She rolled her eyes at me, then turned her attention back to Callie.

"Look, I'm ready to go. I had a run in with Addison and he blew mines," she sighed.

"Fine. Trench, I'll get up with you tomorrow or something. Karma, it was nice meeting you," Callie said, getting off the seat.

"Callie, the fuck you think you going ma? My bruh can take your friend home."

"Nigga, don't be offering my services."

"Callie, don't even look over here because I'm not going anywhere with this asshole." I laughed a little when she called me an asshole because I was only dishing what I was given.

"Shawty, you would be lucky if I let yo mean ass in my car."

"Royce, stop acting like that; the both of you are ready to go home, so just let him drop you off," Callie told her.

Royce looked at me, rolled her eyes, then sighed. "Fine. I'll take him up on his offer, but you owe me big time heffa."

"You know I got you, baby." Callie smiled, hugging her girl.

"Come on 'cause I don't got all night," I said interrupting.

"Chill out and be nice to my girl; she had a rough day."

"I'm nice to those who are nice to me. Royce, you ready?" I asked, trying to be a little nicer.

"I guess," she spat, walking towards the door.

Trench and Callie started laughing, but I didn't find shit funny. Royce had a fucking attitude problem and I didn't appreciate the shit. I walked outside, walking right past her ass. I said wassup to a couple of ladies that were outside, then headed for my car.

"You didn't have to walk past me like that to say wassup to your fan club. I wouldn't have got in your way," Royce complained, getting in my car.

"Royce, I don't know what nigga pissed you off, but I'm not the one. I don't have time for your bitchy attitude and shit. All I'm trying to do is be nice and give yo' ass a ride, but you can't even be appreciative," I snapped.

"You don't know me, so don't talk to me that way."

"You're right. I don't know you and I don't wanna get to know you either. Shit, I already know enough about you to make this the last conversation we have. Plug your address in, then just shut up and enjoy the ride."

"You are such a fucking asshole, I swear." She sucked her teeth, then rolled her eyes. She plugged her address in, then leaned back with her arms crossed over her chest. I pushed down on the gas, turning the hour drive into a forty-five minute one. The car ride was silent and I was cool with that. I haven't met not one female that made me want to ring their fucking neck the way Royce had me wanting to ring hers. She was so fucking beautiful, but her demeanor screamed she was broken, which in turn left her with a fucked up attitude.

"Thank you for the ride," Royce said softly, once I pulled up to her building. She went to get out the car when I reached for her arm, stopping her. She turned around and looked at me, waiting for me to explain my actions.

"Don't let what someone has done to you affect who you truly are ma. No need to be bitter behind a nigga when you look that beautiful ight." I didn't know what came over me, but I felt like she deserved to hear those kind words.

She nodded her head yes, then rushed out the car. I watched her fumble with her keys before she pulled it together and unlocked the door. Instead of driving away as soon as she got in the house, I stayed parked outside for a second. I don't know what it was but something wasn't allowing me to drive off, leaving her in the house alone. I took a deep breath because what I was about to do was going against everything I believed in.

I dialed Trench's number, hoping he was still at the party with Callie.

"Yo!" he yelled over the music and into the phone.

"Put Callie on the phone."

"Hol' on."

"Hello."

"Callie, what's your girl's number?"

"What do you want with her number? You were just with her; why didn't you ask for it?" she asked, sounding skeptical.

"You let your friend get in my car without a problem, but you wanna question me about getting her number. Just give me the shit."

Callie went on and on about how I better not hurt her girl or anything like that. Everything she was saying went in one ear and out the other; a nigga wasn't trying to hear nothing but seven numbers. She eventually gave me Royce's number damn near ten minutes later. I dialed the number, waiting for her to pick up the phone.

"Hello?"

"Come back outside."

"Who is this. Karma?"

"Come back outside," I repeated myself again.

"What are you still doing outside? Do I need to call the police?"

"Royce, you and I both know I'm not a stalker, so bring your ass outside and stop with all the fucking dramatics."

"Okay," she said and hung up the phone. I ran my hands over my waves, trying to figure out what the fuck I was doing.

Chapter 5: Royce

Even though I agreed to go back outside, I wasn't sure if I actually wanted too. To be honest, the only thing I wanted to do was eat some cookies and cream ice cream and put on a good romance movie. Being social wasn't supposed to be on the agenda for the day but, of course, Callie and my mother thought the best way to get over a guy was to find a new one. Callie is my best friend and I love her to death, but she didn't know anything about heart break because her heart has never been broken. All throughout college, Callie remained single, only dealing with a guy when it was beneficial to her. If a dude wasn't offering her something, then they weren't worth her time of day. Most people called her a gold digger; Callie called it knowing what she wanted. I never judged her because at the end of the day, who am I to judge her actions?

A text came through on my phone from Karma, telling me I got two minutes to get outside before he came in. I rushed upstairs to Callie's room to change into something more comfortable. I didn't know Karma at all, so I wasn't going to give him my address. Instead, I gave him Callie's. I was grateful that the many times I slept over here, I left clothes behind because if I didn't, I wouldn't have anything to change into. Callie and I were literally like night and day. I stood five feet even with a rich chocolate complexion, Callie was 5'9" with a soft butter pecan skin tone. Where I was thick, she was skinny; she wore twenty-two-inch weave while I rocked my natural hair. We were complete opposites but somehow, we made it work.

I quickly changed into my capri joggers with an off the shoulder crop top and slipped my feet into my Air Max 95's. I checked myself in the mirror, making sure I looked decent. The ponytail my hair was in was still intact and I was glad. Rubbing my Esos lip balm against my lips, I grabbed my phone and keys, heading back to the front door.

"You lucky yo ass came out when you did 'cause I was about to fuck this door up to get to you," Karma said. He was the first thing I saw once I opened the door.

"No need to fight the door; I was coming out." I giggled.

This awkward silence fell upon us as the cool air blew in our direction. I closed the door and sat on the front steps, just enjoying the cool breeze. Karma eventually joined me. The way he was staring at me caused me to feel a little self-conscience. His eyes were piercing into my soul, giving me a feeling I never felt before. I shifted a little, trying to regain my composure.

"Wassup Butta?" he asked, breaking the silence.

"I don't know. You're the one that told me to come back outside. And why do you feel the need to keep calling me Butta?"

"What's your story?" I asked her, ignoring her question about me calling her Butta.

"Who said I have a story?" I was a little offended by his question, but I tried my best not to let it show.

"Anyone who looks into your eyes can see you got a story to tell, not to mention that snappy ass attitude."

"I'm sorry for how I was acting towards you back at the party. I didn't mean anything by it; today just isn't my day." There was no real reason on why I snapped at Karma, besides me taking my frustrations out on him instead of Addison.

"You don' even got to apologize ma. Just tell me what nigga got you down and shit?"

"Why would I tell you my problems when I don't even know you?"

"Sometimes it's easier to tell a stranger your problems because they just listen without judgment."

"You just may be right."

"Nah, you know I'm right so get to talking." He smiled slightly, causing his dimples to form.

"I don't even know where to begin. Yesterday, well two days ago now, seeing how it's two in the morning." An uneasy laugh escaped my mouth as I tried to find the right words to explain my situation.

"Anyway, I caught my boyfriend of six years in the bed with another chick and, this morning, he showed up at my house and that's when I ended things. Tonight, he was at the party since he was the promotor and I got into it with who I guess to be his new girlfriend. It just hurts, you know. I know it's cliché to say that he is all I knew, but it's the truth. We didn't have a perfect relationship, mostly due to his cheating, but I still stuck by his side. I can't tell you the reason I stayed because I honestly don't have one. It wasn't because I was insecure or that I felt as though I needed him. Every time I would try to walk away, it was like gravity would pull me back. The attraction between the two of us was evident, but I think that's all it really was between us. We had the physical but nothing else seemed to follow into the relationship besides hurt and disappointment."

"What made you finally leave?"

"Like I said, I caught him in bed with another female. All the other times he cheated, I found out because the other woman told me or there would be rumors. This time, I caught him in our bed with another chick. That was the finally straw for me. Hearing your man is cheating and see your man cheating are two different things. One is a suspicion and the other is confirmation. I had my confirmation and chose to no longer play the fool."

"I would say I know how you feel but that's a lie because I don't. What I can say is I commend your strength for finally leaving ma. I know leaving the one you love can't be easy," Karma said, placing his hand on my thigh.

"It's not easy and what's sad is that I still love him. My heart still yearns for him and my body still lusts for his touch. I know he is no good for me and, yet, I still want him in a sense." I laughed a little. "Enough about my sad story; tell me a little about you?" I needed to change the subject because the more I talked about my feelings for Addison, the more I got the urge to pick up the phone and call him.

"There's not much to tell." He laughed.

"Lies, how do you expect me to believe that when your eyes are telling me something different."

"Whatever, my eyes are telling you it's a lie," he joked. "Nah, honestly, there isn't much to tell because I live a real simple life."

"Then tell me something about you that no one else knows."

"Why would I tell you something like that?" he questioned with his eyebrow raised.

"Why wouldn't you?"

"Listen, anything I tell you 'bout me will be something someone doesn't know. Never tell everyone everything. The less the people around you know, the better."

"I guess." I laughed.

"Your laugh is pretty as hell. You should do that more often."

"Do what?"

"Laugh."

"I would but a broken heart isn't easy to repair," I sighed, feeling emotional all over again.

"It is if you find the right one to mend it." He cupped my chin, looking deep into my eyes.

"So, what are you saying? You want to mend my heart?" I spoke just above a whisper. This moment we were in was intimate, yet innocent.

"Hello, no, your attitude is too much for a nigga like me. The way you be sassin' off at the mouth, I might end up choking the shit out of your little ass." He laughed, mushing me softly.

I stuck up my middle finger at him and joined in his laughter. "It's getting late. I'm about to go inside," I told him, standing up.

"Ight shawty, stay up ight. That fuck nigga isn't worth your tears and you're too pretty to be stressed."

"Thanks." I smiled. I waved goodbye, then quickly went into the house.

∞ ∞ ∞

"Last night was a movie," Callie gushed as we sat at the kitchen table eating breakfast. It was two in the afternoon and we were just now waking up. I nodded my head agreeing, as I shoved some eggs into my mouth.

"Yeah, it was cool. I didn't know you were seeing someone."

"Girl, who am I seeing?"

"You and Trench seemed a little buddy buddy."

"I met his ass last night, we danced a little, then went over to the bar to take some shots. Nothing even jumped off. He was offering to buy me drinks and I was accepting."

"Uh huh, if that's what you want to call it."

"Enough about me; what happened with you and Karma? One minute he is being an asshole, then he's calling to get your number."

"Wait, he called you to get my number?"

"Yeah, he called Trench then asked for me. How else did you think he got it?"

"It didn't even register to me that he called my phone honestly and nothing happened between us. All we did was talk."

"Shit, you better than me because I would've done more than just talked. Karma is beyond fine."

"I bet you would've with your hot ass."

"Mhmm, don't hate because I sample the dick, instead of being tied down by the dick. Now that you're single, you should get down with the crown."

"I'll pass." I laughed. Yeah, I was single but that didn't mean I was going to jump in bed with just anyone. I still had standards and I still believed in love.

"Anywho, let's go outside and get into something. It's the weekend; we need to turn up."

"Even if it wasn't the weekend, you would want to turn up. Did you think about doing summer classes?" The spring semester was almost over and the summer one would be here before we knew it. Originally, I was going to take summer classes but with all the Addison stress, I could use a semester off.

"I was thinking about it but I don't know. What about you?"

"I'm taking the semester off. I think I just need to take time to get myself together and find me again."

"Oh shit, then I'm taking the semester off too. We will use this summer to reinvent ourselves."

"I like the sound of that."

"Good. Now let's get dressed, so we can start our day."

We cleaned up the kitchen, then hurried to get dress to see what the day would bring. For a while, we just walked around the hood Callie lived in, but after a while, it started to get boring.

"We need to find something to do because walking around the hood isn't what I had planned for my night," I told Callie.

"Stop complaining. I just want to chill and see what's going on. Maybe we might hear about a party or something."

"You and I both know that's a lie. But come with me in this store right quick. I want a Pepsi."

There were a couple of dudes in front of the store but that was nothing new. We walked in the store and it was packed. Dudes were all in the store posted up, while the females stood in their bird stance trying to get their attention.

"Let's walk a couple of blocks to the next corner store," I told Callie.

"Why would we do that when we are already at this one?"

"It's packed as hell in here and you know I don't care to be around too many people."

"Girl, just go get your damn soda." Callie laughed, pushing me in the direction of the fridge.

In order for me to get to the fridge, I had to push my way through about four niggas. They all tried to stop and talk to me, but I paid them no mind. I finally got my soda and went to the front to pay.

"1.50," the dude behind the counter said.

"It's cool Butta, keep yo money." Without looking at the person, I already knew who it was that paid for my soda. I grabbed it off the counter, along with a straw, and walked outside with Callie.

"Hol' up Butta. I could've sworn I just bought you that soda," Karma said.

I stopped walking and turned around. What I saw caught me off guard because I didn't remember Karma looking this good. He was tall as shit with smooth caramel looking skin. His hair was in a dark ceasar with his waves on swim. He was dressed in jeans and a hoodie, but dude looked good as hell. He must of caught on to me checking him out because a smirk spread across his face, showing off his dimples.

"You bought someone named Butta a soda and for the life of me, I don't know who that is," I sassed. He walked closer to me as Callie stood off to the side.

"Why you playing with me? You know your name is Butta."

"Why do you insist on calling me that?" I quizzed.

"I don't know, chalk it up to your soft ass skin," he smirked, caressing my cheek. "On another note, I think I deserve a thank you."

"Nah, I don't see how you got that," I joked.

"You a rude lil one, you know that Butta."

"I might have been told that a time or two." I lightly chuckled. "I'm only joking; thank you for the soda Karma." I smiled and turned to walk away.

"Girl, that nigga is too fine," Callie said, grabbing my arm as we walked down the block.

"Last night, I thought he was just cute but seeing him in the daylight had me ready to call him daddy." I smiled back.

"Wait, is this Royce speaking or Butta speaking?" Callie enthused.

"Oh shut up. I don't know why he calls me that anyway."

"I think it's cute Butta," Callie teased.

This was the second time I ran into Karma, and I was glad I did. It was something about him that seemed different, yet the same. It was hard to explain but being in his presence did something to me.

Chapter 6: Karma

I watched Butta walk away as she put something extra in her stride. I smirked because she was trying to bait a nigga. If she wanted to put it out there, who was I not to get hooked. I jumped in my car and drove to the corner, cutting her and her friend off from crossing the street. I rolled down the window with a smile on my face.

"Come get in the car," I told them.

"You could've killed us and now you want us to get in the car?" Butta sassed.

"You still breathing right? That means you straight then. Get in the car ma."

Butta looked at her friend, then her friend looked at me. "Where are you taking us?" she asked.

"You chilling with me for the night. Nothing is going to pop off and as long as you're with me, then you straight." They both looked a little skeptical. I chuckled, then put their worry at ease. "Look, y'all got my word I'm not on no funny shit. We taking a trip to the Bronx."

"Why we going out there?" her friend asked.

"That's where I be at," I told her simply.

"Then, what are you doing out in Brooklyn?" Butta questioned.

"I usually don't do this whole twenty-one questions shit but if you must know, I don't live where I be and I don't be where I live."

They both were looking at me confused as hell. I laughed and parked because I was holding up traffic. I jumped out the car and walked towards them.

"Forgive me, but what's your name again lil mama?" I asked the friend.

"Callie."

"Callie, get in my car right quick while I talk to Butta."

I tossed her the key, so she could get inside. I started taking steps towards Butta, backing her into the wall of some building.

"Karma, what are you doing?" she asked, looking me in the eyes.

I stared back at her with intensity to see if she was going to look away. She never did, causing me to nod my head in approval. I had this thing about eye contact. If a person couldn't look me in the eye, that meant they were bitch made and I couldn't fuck with a person like that.

"Karma, I don't scare easily, so you looking at me like that isn't doing nothing for me," she smirked. Her deep dimples became visible and I couldn't help but to stick my finger in the right one.

"Why you making shit hard, like I'm some rapist nigga or something?" I asked her.

"How you pull up on the block while we are trying to cross the street? You could've caused a whole accident."

"My bad about that, but I wasn't tryin' to kill you or nothing. I'm just trying to get your attention."

"That's all you had to say." She smiled, then strutted over to my car. She got in the passenger seat, then rolled down the window. "Are you going to stand there or are you going to come on?"

I laughed a little, then swaggered over to the car. Getting in, I pulled off and threw in a cd that I made with all my favorite Jigga songs. The first track was one of my favorites. I turned the volume up as Jay started spittin' them bars.

Too many faggot niggas clocking my spending. Exercising your gay like minds like Richard Simmons. If you could catch Jay right, on the late night. Without the eight, right, maybe you could test my weight, right. I dip, spit quicker than you ever seen. Administer pain, next the minister's screaming your name. At your wake as I peek in, look in your casket, feeling sarcastic, 'look at him, still sleeping.' You never ready, forever petty minds stay petty. Mine's thinking longevity until I'm seventy. Living heavenly, fuck felony after felony what? Nigga you broke, what the fuck you going to tell me?"

I looked over at Butta, nodding her head and mouthing the words to the song. "What you know about this?"

"Callie, tell this man that I'm forever a Jay Z fan." She laughed.

"Please don't get her started on his ass," Callie said from the back.

"Ight, spit a verse for me." The verse she rhymed would tell me if she was a true fan or not.

"I don't have to prove my love for Jay Z to you or anyone else," she sassed.

"Man, it ain't even that serious; get yo panties out the crack of your ass. Just spit something Butta, damn."

"I guess." She rolled her eyes, then started rapping. "A face of stone was shocked on the other end of the phone. Word back home is that you had a special friend. So, what was oh so special then? You have given away without getting at me. That's your fault, how many times you forgiven me? How was I to know that you was plain sick of me? I know the way a nigga living was whack, but you don't get a nigga back like that. Shit, I'm a man with pride, you don't do shit like that. You don't just pick up and leave and leave me sick like that. You don't throw away what we had, just like that. I was just fucking them girls, I was gon' get right back. They say you can't turn a bad girl good, but once a good girl's gone, she's gone forever. I mourn forever, shit. I've got to live with the fact I did you wrong forever."

I listened to her flow and she was ight. "With a little work, you could be the next up and coming rapper. But *Song Cry* is a generic song; everyone and they mama know that song."

"This shit is wicked on these mean streets. None of my friends speak, we're all tryna win. But then again, maybe it's for the best though. Cause when they're saying too much. You know they're trying to get you touched. Whoever said illegal was the easy way out, couldn't understand. The mechanics and the workings of the underworld, granted. Nine to five is how you survive, I ain't trying to survive. I'm tryna live it to the limit and love it a lot. Life ills poisoned my body. I used to say fuck mic skills. I never prayed to God, I prayed to Gotti. That's right it's wicked, that's life I live it. Ain't asking for forgiveness for my sins, ends. I break bread with the late heads. Picking their brains for angles on, all the evils that the game'll do. It gets dangerous, money and power is changing us. And now we're lethal, infected with D'evils."

When she spit the first verse from D'evils, which was on Jay Z's first album, I knew she was the truth.

"Ight Butta, you redeemed yo self with that one."

"Nigga, I did the damn thing; you don't have to front." She laughed.

"Y'all are so annoying, play some Lil Wayne or something," Callie said.

"Nah," I said, shaking my head and laughing. We vibed out to the rest of my Jay Z cd; Butta and I took turns rapping each song back to back. The whole car ride was love and if I wasn't digging her little feisty ass before, I was trying to fuck with her now.

∞ ∞ ∞

Pulling up to the spot, I got out and led the way to an empty apartment I sometimes crashed at when I wanted to keep an eye on my spots. I used my key to unlock the door and stepped to the side, so they could walk in. The apartment was furnished and clean as fuck because the only time anyone was over here was in between shifts when it was time for niggas to eat. I made sure the kitchen was always stocked because eating or drinking at the trap wasn't allowed. The trap was for work and nothing more. A nigga wasn't going to catch the itis and get caught slipping,

"This is where you live?" Callie asked.

"Nah, this is just where I be. There's food in the kitchen and drinks in the fridge. Make y'all self at home; I'll be right back."

I walked out the apartment and casually went to the staircase. I climbed the stairs two at a time, going two floors up. I went to apartment 6D and let myself in.

"Damn nigga, I thought you were going to be here two hours ago," Trench said.

"Don't clock me, nigga. But yo, Smitty, what the lick read?" I asked. Smitty was our top worker in Mott Haven. Whenever Trench or I wasn't around, Smitty held shit down. If I was to ever move up, Smitty would definitely be the dude to take over for me.

"Everything is everything my G," he said, nodding his head.

"Cool. Trench, come with me right quick."

"You just got here and you tryin' to leave already nigga."

"Bosses don't punch clocks."

"Touché my nigga, touché. Smitty, make sure the count is A1 before you wrap up tonight."

"I got you, Trench. I'm not new to this; no need to repeat shit that I already know," Smitty told Trench.

"Ight Youngin', you got it."

We both dapped up Smitty then left out. On the way downstairs to the apartment where Butta and Callie was at, I filled Trench in on the girls. Walking in the apartment, both Callie and Butta had their feet on the coffee table with their shoes kicked off. Sodas along with a bag of chips were on the coffee table, causing me to laugh.

"Y'all didn't waste no time getting comfortable. How y'all got your stinkin' ass feet on the coffee table next to the chips?" I snatched the bag from off the coffee table and dug in.

"Nobody's feet over here is stinkin'; you must be talking about your own," Butta said.

"If that's your truth, then who am I to knock it. Y'all already know Trench from last night, right," I introduced.

"What's up Butta?"

"The name is Royce," Butta told him.

"Like Rolls Royce?" he asked with laughter in his voice.

"Yeah, is there a problem with that?" she sassed.

"Nah shawty, not at all, chill out. Wassup Callie."

"Nothing much." Callie smiled. Trench and Callie were staring at each other hard as fuck. From the looks of it, they were ready to get into something.

"Butta, come fuck with me in the back," I told her.

"Uh why?" she asked.

"Ain't nothing gonna pop off; just let me talk to you right quick."

She didn't look like she was going to move anytime soon, leaving me no choice but to move her ass myself. I picked her up off the couch, bringing her into the room.

"You didn't have to throw me," she complained once she landed on the bed.

"You the one that didn't want to walk on your own and shit."

"That's because I was trying to figure out why you wanted me in here to begin with."

"Relax because shit isn't even popping like that. My dick too elite for you, Butta."

"Why do you keep calling me Butta when my name is Royce."

"Are you hard of hearing? I already told you to chalk it up to your soft ass skin." I shrugged. I didn't know why I called her that; just seemed like it fit when I touched her hand that night at the party.

"Yeah whatever." She giggled.

"Just shut up and find something for us to watch."

I handed her the remote and sat in the chair that was in the corner of the room. The Wayne Brothers was on and I was cool watching that. For the rest of the night, we just chilled with each other. I ended up ordering pizza for us because she was hungry. While we ate, we talked about a few things. Not much was said between the two of us; the little that was said gave me a glimpse into the world of Royce. She told me all about her mother and how close they were and even touched on school. For the most part, she was cool, chilling with her was like chilling with my nigga in a sense. She wasn't all worried about how she looked and she damn sure didn't care about eating in front of me. She bust down ten wings without even missing a beat. The way I was dealing with Butta was out of the norm for me. Granted, I only known her for about twenty-four hours; if this was any other chick, I would've hit by now and been back to the money chase. Butta had me thinking she might just be the real deal.

Chapter 7: Royce

"Royce wake up!" I heard Callie yelling.

"What time is it?" I yawned, all the while trying to wipe the sleep out my eye.

I didn't remember when I fell asleep, but I knew it couldn't have been that long ago. Karma and I stayed up watching tv. He seemed cool but, at the same time, he came across as guarded. Not once did he mention his family or anything. He really wasn't even talking; he just listened.

"It's three in the afternoon," Callie said, getting in the bed with me.

"Damn, I need to get home. I know my mom is probably blowing up my phone." Callie reached over, passing me my phone and just like I knew, I had missed calls and numerous texts from my mother. I sent her back a text letting her know that I would be home soon.

"Where are the guys?" It didn't hit me that Karma wasn't in the room with me until now.

"I don't even know. I just woke up myself and they were gone."

"Well, let's get out of here because I don't think this is either one of their cribs."

We grabbed all of our stuff and headed for the door. Just as we were about to walk out, Karma and Trench were about to walk in.

"Damn, I leave you alone for an hour or so and you already trying to leave. What you gonna do when shit start getting real? I thought you were the type to hold a nigga down." Karma lightly pushed me back into the house. It was crazy because for some reason, it felt as though we were the only people around.

"I am the type to hold my dude down; the funny thing is you're not my dude," I smirked.

"Yeah whatever, just eat this McGriddle I got you." He passed me the bag and went to sit on the couch.

"You didn't get sausage or bacon on it, right?" I didn't care for pork too much.

"What you thought when you were talking last night I didn't hear you?"

"I mean, who knows? Y'all dudes only hear what y'all want to hear," I told him, unraveling my breakfast.

"It's kind of hard to block you out when your voice is squeaky as fuck."

"Fuck you." I stuck up my middle finger for more emphasis.

"It's on you, Butta. Just give me a time and a place." I rolled my eyes at him because he was never getting this.

Callie came over to the table and sat across from me, eating her breakfast. Karma and Trench went in the living room with their bag of food.

"Wassup with you and Trench?" I asked her.

"Nothing." She shrugged and I gave her ass a knowing look. "We didn't do anything, if that's what you're asking."

"That's not what I was asking, but it's good to know."

"He seems cool, but you know how I get down. If a dude isn't investing in me, then he has to go."

"I can understand that," I told her.

We finished the rest of our food in silence because there was a funny vibe in the room. Whenever I would look towards the living room, Trench would be side eyeing me. I didn't know what his problem was, but he was rubbing me the wrong way. I couldn't have been happier when Callie and I finished eating, and Karma told us he had something to handle.

While Callie was saying her goodbyes to Trench, Karma and I headed towards his car.

"When am I going to see you again?" he asked me, leaning me against his car.

"I don't know; I guess whenever our paths should cross."

"Don't tell me that bullshit Butta. When am I going to see you again?"

"Karma, I don't know. I just got out of something and you know how that goes."

Before he could respond, Callie came over to us and got in the car. Karma walked away from me and headed towards his side of the car. It was like Karma caught a slight attitude because I couldn't give him a direct answer. I went to slip into the backseat with Callie, but Karma deaded that quick.

"Butta, get in the front and stop playing," Karma said, stopping me. I looked at him as if to say yeah right and went to slide in.

"Royce, you heard what I said. I'm not the type that repeats himself." When he said my name, it sent a chill that went straight to my honey pot. I closed the door and jumped in the passenger seat. I made sure to suck my teeth, so he would know I didn't appreciate the way he just talked to me.

"I see you listen when I call you Royce." He laughed, pulling off.

"Whatever Karma."

The ride back to Callie's house was a quiet one. No one was saying anything, which made it a little awkward. When Karma pulled up, Callie was the first one out the car.

"Thanks for the ride Karma." She smiled before heading towards her building. He nodded his head, then turned his attention to me.

"Thanks for the ride," I told him, ready to get out.

"So, you just gonna get out my car without giving me a kiss or telling me when I'm going to see you again."

"I told you, Karma; I just got out of a situation."

"Man, what you had going on with that nigga is y'all business. The hurt he caused you needs to be left with that nigga. In a matter of twenty-four hours, you have done something that no other chick has been able to do."

"And what exactly is that?" I questioned.

"You been able to keep me interested; you might not know it, but that's something to brag about."

"Oh, it's something I could brag about, huh?"

"Yeah, I don't pay these hoes half the attention I showed you." He laughed, but I didn't find it funny at all.

"That's your problem; you too busy messing with these hoes."

"So, tell me who I should be fucking with?" He licked his lips slightly, which caused me to laugh.

"Stop trying to lick yo lips like cool James, play boy. I can't tell you the type of chick you need because I don't know you. What I can tell you is that you won't get nowhere messing with these hoes. Hoes are only around for the money and the moment. What happens when the moment and the money is gone? They move on to the next. If that's the type of life you want to live, then by all means, it's your life."

"What if the life I want to live involves you? What if I want to take all your hurt and carry it as my own? What if I want to come into your world and turn it upside down? What if I want to fuck you silly? What if I want to fuck yo mental, then lick the juices from yo pussy? What if I want to get you all in yo feelings? Would you allow me too?"

"Only time will tell," I told him, getting out the car and speed walking towards my building. This nigga didn't do anything but ask some simple questions and he had me caught up.

I entered my building and that's when I heard Karma calling after me. *Shit,* I cursed under my breath. I turned around to see what he wanted but made sure to put my key in the door.

"You ran out the car so fast, you left yo phone on the seat. Did those simple questions fuck you up that bad Butta?" He laughed.

"No, they didn't fuck me up and thank you for my phone," I sassed, rolling my eyes.

"You know I can make yo eyes roll, if that's the type of shit you like." He smirked.

He started walking towards me, causing me to drop my keys. It didn't make no damn sense how bad he had my nerves whenever he was around me.

"Karma, what do you think you're doing?" I complained.

"Shhhhh," he whispered. He pulled me to him and bent down, placing his lips on mine.

This wasn't my first kiss, but this was the best kiss I ever had. His soft lips against mine did something to me. I gently sucked on his tongue as he whirled it around in my mouth. His hands rested at my hips while his pelvis was pressed against mine. The kiss wasn't freaky; it was more so intimate. Just as I was getting deeper into the kiss, Karma pulled away.

"I put my number in yo phone, make sure you use that shit," he told me as he stepped away. I wasn't able to form words, so I just nodded my head. I walked to the door, lightly touching my lips because it felt as though Karma's lingered against mine still. A smile crept on my face as I unlocked the door. Karma was strange as hell, but it allured me to him. I was definitely going to use his number because I needed to find out what ole boy was about.

Chapter 8: Karma

A nigga was tired after counting money all day; all I wanted was some food and my bed and I would be straight. I had been over in the hood handling business for the last week. Butta had crossed my mind a couple of times, but a nigga just didn't have a moment to text her or to call just to see what's up. Yeah, Royce had my attention but money will always be my first love. I got it by any means and that just wasn't a statement; it was a fact. Where I am now in this game has everything to do with hard work and dedication. I gave my life to this game just to maintain and, now, all a nigga had to do was sit back and watch the money roll in, but that's not what I did.

I never touched the drugs, but I didn't trust a soul to count my money. Smitty would collect everything at the end of every day and bring it to me to count. Trench was my man, a hundred grand, and I wouldn't let him touch the money. I guess I was just weird or some shit. But I didn't care to have someone else come to me and tell me that my money was coming up short. Nah, if my money came up short, then a nigga was getting handled and replaced. I didn't give out second chances. You cross me once and it's lights out. Whatever I came up short on, I would just replace. Red would never have to hear about the money being short because by the time it got to him, everything would be straight. I only had one incident where my money came up short. I made sure to kill that nigga Mooks in front of the whole team. That nigga died at the hands of everyone in the crew. I made each person stab Mooks' ass until he was no longer breathing. I needed these niggas to know that I wasn't out here playing. A nigga had a job and one job only; get that money.

"Everything is everything. I'm 'bout to get up out of here and head to the crib," I told Trench and Smitty.

"Hol' up. I want to talk to you 'bout something," Trench said.

"Wassup nigga."

"I need you to chill out here tonight."

"Tonight is your night to hold shit down." Since our traps were on that twenty-four-hour shit, Trench and I alternated weeks where we would stay in Mott Haven, just to make sure shit was straight and nothing went down.

"I know but something came up and I need to handle that."

"Nigga, you need to come with a better reason than that."

"Damn, you act like you can't cover for a nigga off the strength of my word."

"I don't like switching shit up and you know it. When you switch things up last minute, you look unorganized and when shit starts to look unorganized, niggas start to feel like they can fall out of line," I told him.

"And if they fall out of line, then they get handled."

"The objective is to get that money up, not yo body count."

"If I let you tell it. I'm tryin' to take Callie out and see what's up with her."

"So, you stoppin' for some… you know what? Forget it, you good nigga," I told him, shaking my head.

"Then you holdin' shit down for me?"

"Yeah, I got you, nigga."

I dapped him up, then told Smitty to hit me if he needed anything. I went to the spare apartment and looked for something to cook. All the meat was frozen, which left me assed out. I was about to say fuck it and take my ass to sleep when Butta crossed my mind once again. I pulled out my phone and sent her a text, telling her to call me. A couple of seconds later, a text came through on my phone.

Butta:

Y would u text me just 2 tell me 2 call.

I laughed at the text, then put my phone back in my pocket. Not even five minutes later, my phone was ringing. I let that shit go to voicemail and jumped in the bed. Flicking through the channels, an episode of Law & Order: SVU was on. I sat the remote down and as soon as I got into the show, my phone started ringing.

"Yo!" I answered, already knowing who was on the other line.

"Why would you text me telling me to call when the time you used to send the text, you could've just called," Butta sassed.

"Why would you text me back, instead of calling like I asked? We can go back and forth with the questions but that's not going to getting either one of us anywhere. But, wassup, how you been?"

"I been okay really, just trying to focus on finishing out school with a strong gpa. I decided to not take summer classes, so I'm going to take the summer to really find myself again."

"That sounds dope as hell."

"Yeah."

"What you doin' tonight? I kinda miss ya short ass."

"Yeah right because if you missed me, then you would've picked up the phone to send a text or call."

"I did pick up the phone to send a text, so what you saying?" I laughed.

"True but it was a whole week later."

"The phone works two ways sweetheart. If you wanted to talk to me, all you had to do was send that text and I would've came running."

"I doubt you would've came running."

"You're right. I would've took my time, but I would've met you nonetheless. So, what's up? You wanna chill out with me tonight?"

"I would, but I have somewhere to be around eleven."

"The fuck you going at eleven? Ain't shit open but trap houses and legs." Hearing that she had somewhere to be so late at night pissed me all the way off.

"Um, I think you need to calm down a little because I'm not even that type of girl."

"Yeah but that's not telling me where you're going either."

"I'm going down to the Cracked Mug, if you must know."

"Ight, then I'll come with you. It's only seven now so come over and we can have dinner together, then once we done, we can head over to the Cracked Mug. You just have to cook for a nigga."

"Wait, you want me to come to where you at and cook?"

"That's exactly what I want you to do. Why you acting like what I just asked you for was a hard request?"

"Whatever Karma. I hope you're picking me up."

"I need you to go to the supermarket and pick up something quick to cook; all the meat in the crib is frozen. I'll pay for your cab."

"You're asking for a lot," she sighed.

"I'll make it up to you, ight."

"I don't know how you're going to make it up to me, but I guess. I'll text you when I'm leaving the supermarket, so you can send me your address."

"Bring an overnight bag too," I added, just to see if she would go for it.

"I don't even know why you would ask that." She laughed, then hug up the phone.

I smirked then rested against my headboard. Butta was something else but everything about her piqued my interest.

∞ ∞ ∞

"You are so lucky cooking is something that I like to do or you would be starving," Butta said, handing me my plate.

"You would leave your baby hungry?"

"What baby? I don't have a man or no kids."

"Yeah ight, you spoken for, know that," I told her, meaning every word. I wasn't sure what I was looking for with Butta, but I knew wasn't no other nigga gonna be stepping to her. Call me selfish; I would claim that shit.

I watched her strut back into the kitchen, grabbing her plate. She came and sat on the couch next to me. No words were said between the two of us as we indulged in our philly cheese steak sliders. These little shits were good as fuck. When I finished the three I had, I went in the kitchen to get some more.

"Damn, I know I can cook but I didn't think I cooked that good." She laughed when I sat back down.

"A nigga is just hungry, that's all."

"Yeah whatever. You want something to drink?"

"Yeah, pass me a bottle of water."

She got up, grabbed her plate, and went off into the kitchen. I assumed she was cleaning everything up from her cooking because it took her a little while to come back into the living room. She passed me a bottle of water, then opened her own and drank some. When she removed the bottle from her mouth, a couple of drops slipped down her mouth. I reached over, softly caressing her chin. Her body froze from my touch while my body demanded I move in closer. I cupped her chin, bringing her face closer to mine. My dick was all the way active from the way she was staring at me. She had this angelic look on her face that made me want to give her any and everything she felt she deserved.

"Uh, what do you think you're doing?" Butta asked as we exchanged breaths.

"Royce," I whispered, looking deep into her eyes.

"Yes," she whispered back.

"Your breath smells like straight shit." I laughed, mushing her away.

"My breath doesn't stink; you must've been smelling your own breath," she pouted, sticking up the middle finger.

"Don't be upset Butta. I got an extra toothbrush and some toothpaste in the bathroom. Go handle that, then I'll suck on them juicy lips."

"Your mouth isn't getting anywhere near mine. Hurry up, so we can get to the club. It's out in Queens," she sassed but got up and headed to the bathroom.

Damn, I was hoping the Cracked Mug was somewhere local because I had to stay close in case something popped off. I pulled out my phone and called Smitty.

"Ayo, I thought yo ass would be sleep by now," he said, answering.

"Nah but yo, I need you to shut shit down for the night. I'm not going to be around."

"Hol' the fuck up; this can't be Karma talkin'. Nigga, who you fucking Beyoncé or some shit. What chick got you ready to miss out on money?"

"Nah, you right, fuck that. I'll just tell her we have to play the crib tonight," I told him and hung up the phone.

"Yo Butta!" I called out.

"Yeah," she said, coming out the bathroom.

"We gonna have to take a rain check on the Cracked Mug tonight."

"Wait what?" From the way her face scrunched up, I could already tell that she was catching an attitude.

"We gonna have to take a rain check. I can't miss out on no money," I told her truthfully.

"Wow, really Karma," she gasped. "Don't worry about it," she snapped.

"What you catching an attitude for because we can't go to some coffee house?"

"My attitude is because you are so fucking stupid. You are filled with nothing but greed and it's a damn shame. You can't come out with me because you are going to miss a couple of dollars. Money isn't even all that important; there are bigger things in life besides money."

"Like what, since you think you know everything?"

"Love is more important than money. Companionship is more important than money. If you don't see that, then that's sad as hell."

"All that shit you just listed is the reason you are heartbroken. You were looking for love and companionship and look how that shit turned out. People can disappoint you and hurt you, while money does nothing but bring you happiness. If you can't understand that, then you need to reevaluate life on some real shit."

"You are absolutely right. Love and companionship is exactly what has me heartbroken, but one thing it didn't do is make me bitter, and that's more than you can say. I don't know who turned you bitter; however, I don't have to deal with it," she spat, then stormed out the house.

As soon as the door slammed, I instantly felt bad about the way I handled things with her. I never gave a fuck about anyone else's feelings besides mine. Royce storming out like that though had me all fucked up. I haven't even known this chick for a month and already she had me going against the fucking grain.

Chapter 9: Royce

"Royce, calm down. Where are you and what happened? Trench, give me a second," Callie said into the phone. As soon as I walked out of Karma's building, I called a cab and walked up the block a little. I wasn't about to stand in front of a hood I didn't know, waiting on the cab. The cab took a while to come, so I called Callie. Come to find out, her ass was on a date with Trench.

"Don't even worry about it. I don't want to interrupt your date. I'm just going to go to the Cracked Mug, then go home and study," I told her, ending the call.

I leaned my head, trying to figure out how I always got caught up with these fucked up dudes. Yeah, I just met Karma and I shouldn't have expected anything from him, but I couldn't help it. The way we just talked the night he dropped me off at Callie's house had me thinking he was different or something, only to find out he was fucking worse than the rest. At least I could say I found out how he truly was before things went any further. After tonight, I was swearing off men until the end of the summer. Karma or no other dude needed to have my attention anyway.

My phone started vibrating as soon as the cab pulled up to the Cracked Mug. I looked down and saw Karma's name flashing across the screen. I sent him straight to voicemail and powered off my phone. There was nothing he could say to fix what he did. I walked in and headed straight for the stage. This go around, I wasn't nerves or anything. I was determined to get what I needed to say out because I wanted to know if it was too much.

"Let's welcome Royce back to the Cracked Mug." The crowd cheered as I began to sing *Treat Me Like Somebody* by Tink. Everything was going good and the crowd was vibing with me as I sung accappella. As the song was nearing its end, I felt someone's eyes burning a hole in me. I searched for the gaze and rolled my eyes when I saw who it was. I stared at Karma intensely as I ended out the song.

"Now, don't be misled by the things that I said in the past. I was young; I was looking for a thrill. That didn't last long. I was in it for the wrong, wrong reason, wrong season, wrong person. 'Cause he just wanted one thing and I just wanted something to smile at and live for and hug on. I'd rather have quality than quantity. Oh, I just want someone that'll keep it real with me. Is that too much? 'Cause I've been on the search and I'm losing my hope. Is that too much? Is that too much? Trying to find love in a world so cold."

I carried out that last note before placing the mic back on the stand. The crowd was cheering as I gave Karma one last look before walking off the stage. Instead of leaving, I decided I was going to stay and listen to the other acts. I ordered a cappuccino and grabbed a table. I wasn't sitting down for more than ten minutes when Karma came swaggering my way. Karma was undeniably fine and if I was just looking for an attractive man, I would give him the time of day. Everything that happened earlier between the two of us showed me the type of mentality he had and I wasn't here for it.

"You did good up there Butta. I didn't know you could sing," Karma said, lightly kissing me on the cheek and sitting down.

"There is a lot of things you don't know about me."

"Ight, what's the problem? I still came out, so why are you mad?"

"Karma, how old are you?" I turned to him asked.

"I'm twenty; what does my age have to do with your attitude?"

"You are old enough to figure out the things you said were rude as hell. Just because you showed up after you canceled doesn't mean I'm going to fall to the ground and worship you."

"Yeah ight," Karma said, getting up and storming away from the table.

I paid him no mind because I wasn't going to kiss his ass, nor was I going to explain to him what he did wrong. Karma was a grown ass man who should know what he did wrong. I don't know what he thought I looked like, but I just wasn't the type to pacify his ass.

∞ ∞ ∞

"Wake up Royce! Why are you still sleeping?" I heard my mother say while gently pushing me.

I stirred a little in my sleep before I fully woke up. "What time is it?"

"Twelve and you know you have a class at two."

"Oh shit," I said, jumping up.

71

"Oh shit is right, but you better watch your mouth in my house. Where did you go last night?"

"I went to a friend's house, then went over to the Cracked Mug to sing. I ended up staying there longer than I was supposed to," I explained.

"I think you should try that again. The only friend you have is Callie, so whose house were you at?"

"This guy I meet ma," I sighed. I was trying to maneuver around my room, grabbing everything I needed to get ready and placing it on my bed. All of my mother's questions weren't doing anything but distracting me.

"Oh, so you meet a guy. What's his name?"

"Karma."

"When do I get to meet Karma?"

"Ma, if you don't mind, now isn't the time to be playing twenty-one questions. I'm trying to get everything ready, so I can make it to class on time and take this final."

"Girl, don't sass me; if you weren't hanging out with your new guy friend, you wouldn't have been so sleepy. I'm going to leave you be for now, but we will be having this conversation later."

"Okay ma."

As she left out my room, I was right behind her heading for the bathroom. After Karma left, I stayed at the coffee shop, just chilling and enjoying the vibes. I ended up leaving around one in the morning. By the time I got home, it was close to three. I knew I should've took a shower last night but instead, I crashed as soon as my body touched the bed. I was now paying for my poor decision making.

I quickly washed up, making sure all the vital parts of my body was clean. Getting out, I dried off and quickly put on my coconut oil lotion. After that, I threw on a pair of under armor tights, along with an oversized sweater, and threw on a pair of sneakers. I rushed to put my hair in a bun and by the time I was done, I had about forty-five minutes to make it to class. Grabbing everything I needed, I rushed to my mother's room to see if she would let me use her car. I was going to make sure that I bought me a car asap because taking all of these cabs was a waste of money.

"The keys are on the dresser; make sure you're back by the time, I have to go to work. You need to invest in a car yourself. You working at the tutoring center at your school, so I know they paying you enough."

"I was just thinking the same thing. I will get one soon; I'll be back way before you have to go to work. I love you, ma." I gave her a quick kiss on her cheek, then rushed out the door. I threw my bag in the passenger seat. I was about to pull out when my phone began vibrating on my lap.

I had two text messages but those were gonna have to wait until I made it to school. I pulled off like a bat out of hell. I made it to campus with ten minutes to spare. As I was walking in to the building, I checked my messages. The first one was from Addison, saying we needed to talk, and the other was from Karma. The one from Karma caught me off guard, seeing how he stormed out on me last night. I deleted the one from Addison, then reread the one Karma sent.

Karma:

Have a great day beautiful

His text was simple, but it made me smile. I tucked my phone in my purse as I found my seat. I was still on the fence about Karma, but the text was really sweet and thoughtful. I made a mental note to text him back after this exam. I then blocked everything that wasn't related to this Trigonometry test to the back of my mind. After this exam, I only had one left, and if I passed both of them, I would be done with my junior year in college.

Chapter 10: Karma

"Why you keep lookin' at yo phone while I'm talking to you, young blood?" Red asked.

"Nah nothing," I said, tucking my phone back in my pocket. I couldn't even deny. Royce had my ass feeling like a straight bitch. I sent her a text, telling her to have a good day. I would've thought she would send a text back, but I guess not. She was probably still mad about that shit that happened last night, but she would be ight.

"Yeah okay. Anyway, I've been noticing how the two of you have been putting in work and I just want to say I'm proud of you lil niggas. Y'all are out here getting it and I respect that shit. Neither one of you are flashy and that's a good thing. So many dudes get in this game, just to have the latest kicks that drop and the nice ass cars that allure gold digging woman. Y'all two, on the other hand, are cut from a different cloth."

"We out here just tryin' to get it by any means," Trench said.

"You already know how I feel. Money is the motive," I added.

"Money being the motive is cool, but there is more to life than just money. Go out and experience love or some shit, have a couple of babies, and get married at some point. Money isn't the only thing that makes the world go round. Yeah, it's a big part of it but so is love. What's the point of having money if you ain't got no one to share it with?"

"Red, you dropping jewels today?" Trench laughed, causing Red to chuckle.

"I wouldn't say I'm dropping jewels; I'm just trying to give y'all something to think about."

"The only thing I'm thinking 'bout is making it to the top. The goal is to be sitting where you are one day, Red. You're my inspiration."

"Nah, don't ever call me an inspiration because I don't inspire shit. I let so much shit pass me by because I was on the money chase. Yeah, I have cash money, cars, and hoes but that shit is nothing. Having someone in your corner that's genuinely rooting for you because they care and not because of the shit you have is the shit you should inspire to have. If a person would've told me the shit I'm trying to kick to you little niggas, then I probably wouldn't even still be in this business.

Being forty and still in the game isn't something that I want for y'all. I want y'all niggas to be better than me. Shit, go out and experience all the things I didn't get to experience and be the nigga I didn't get to be."

"I don't know about all of that. For me, the fast life is where it's at." Trench shrugged.

"You say that shit now, until you end up in jail or six feet under. Everything I'm spittin' is just shit I want for y'all. I can want it for y'all all I want, but if the two of you don't want it for y'all selves, then I'm doing nothing but wasting my breath. Got a nigga in here feeling like y'all daddy and shit."

Trench and Red went back and forth while I just sat thinking about all the shit Red was saying. I never thought about it until this moment, but I never seen Red with the same chick. He switched his bitches twice a day. Red and I were close; he was like a father figure to me, so whenever he told me anything, I took that shit into consideration.

"Ayo Trench, let me holla at Karma right quick."

"You want me to wait for you or you good?" Trench asked.

"Nah, I'm good. I'll be by the spot later to make sure shit is what it need to be."

"Ight. It's been real Red," Trench said before leaving out.

"Wassup Red, what you want to talk about?" I asked.

"Why you were so quiet while I was talkin'?"

"Nothing, I was just listening."

"Ya boy don't seem to understand where I'm coming from. He thinks this fast life is where it's at."

"Trench is his own man and believes what he wants."

"What do you believe?"

"You already know for me it was money first, all that other shit second. Love was never an option for me nor was it a thought. You already know my past; the bitch that carried me for nine months didn't even love me enough to stick around. So, how the hell am I supposed to love a woman?"

"Just because you lacked love from a female doesn't mean you can't give a female love. The same way you love this money is the same way you love ya bitch. Just make sure she's that bitch and not some bird bitch. Givin' your love to the wrong chick can be dangerous."

"How would you know when you never been in love?"

"I fucked enough women to know how they operate. They are emotional by nature. Not to mention, love is the only thing they really looking for in a nigga. Now, imagine givin' ya love to a bitch that's just lookin' for a come up. That bitch will make you think she the perfect bitch, ring yo ass dry, then leave you heart broken and cold. Trust my words Karma."

"I hear what you talkin'," I told him.

"That chick that got you closing down shop and checkin' your phone might just be the one."

"I don't know what you talkin' bout."

"Don't try to run game on me because I'm like your father. When you used to hustle on them corners, not once did you leave until you made your quota and even when you made it, you would stay out to make more."

"That's cause a nigga was young and didn't have shit."

"Now, you grown and still don't have shit. Yeah, you have money but that's not shit. If you feeling shawty, then you need to let her know."

"She not even fuckin' with me right now. She mad cause I told her we had to change our plans because I couldn't leave the spot."

"This is Trench's week, so how you get caught up?" Red asked, leaning back in his chair.

"Nigga had a date or some shit. It was nothing for me to cover for him."

"It might have been nothing for you to cover but that nigga got responsibilities. He claims he all about the mighty dollar, but he put that shit on hold for pussy."

"How can you say that about him when I shut shit down for a female?"

"The spot wasn't your responsibility. It was his week to hold shit down, yet he asked you to look out so he could go out to dinner. That shit right there is irresponsible. Trench thinks he got everything figured out but just from talking to him, I already know he ain't fit to take over."

"Trench always holds his own."

"Yeah, the nigga holds his own to prove a point. That nigga is all out for show. The whole time we were talking, the nigga kept referring back to him wanting to be where I am. Trench is just my

79

worker, but he's your boy, so it's natural for you to stick up for him. I see him for what he is."

I wanted to respond, but shit. Who was I to defend another grown ass man? Red and I continued to chop it up until Max walked in.

"Wassup Max," I greeted him out of respect for Red.

"Nigga," he said, then turning his attention to Red.

"Need to talk to you right quick."

"Ight, give me five minutes," Red told him.

Max grilled me all the way to the door. I hit his ass with a smirk because I didn't fear no man.

"You and that nigga need to let what happened at that park go. That shit was five years ago."

"That's ya boy, not me. I don't got no issues with Max but, for some reason, he got issues with me. I'm out of here tho," I told him, getting up.

"Ight, lil nigga, stay up."

We dapped each other up right, then I headed for the door. Red stopped me before I could walk out.

"If she's worth it, then go after her. Don't let a little dumb ass argument stop you from exploring things with her. From what you told me, she already in your head and changing ya mindset. You might as well let her in your heart and unfreeze that thing."

"I hear you," I told him, then left out.

I jumped in my car and sat there for a while, thinking about the conversation I had with Red. He was right about a lot of shit and I honestly wanted to give shit a try with Butta. I just didn't know if I was the type of nigga she need. I wouldn't say she broken but her heart definitely was. She needed help repairing it but, fucking with me, the shit just might end up shredded. I would never hurt her intentionally, but shit happens.

She was dope as fuck though and Red was right. She was already in my head and changing the way I looked at shit. She had me out here doing things that were out the ordinary. I might as well see wassup with her. Just like she would be taking a risk, so would I. *Fuck it, I'm about to get my chick,* I said to myself, as I pulled off.

Chapter 11: Royce

I was on cloud nine as I looked at my posted grade from my exam online. I passed with a ninety-five. Words couldn't explain how happy I was. After the test, I came right home and gave my mother her car. They called her in early for work, so I didn't have time to celebrate or anything. I closed my laptop and sat it over to the side and climbed off my bed. Since I did good on my test, I was about to indulge in one of my guilty pleasures, Talenti Ice Cream. This was the best ice cream I ever had; it was so addictive. I had to eat it in moderations because if I didn't, I would probably look like the cow the milk came from to make the ice cream.

Making my way into the kitchen, I heard the doorbell ring. Rushing over to the door, I was a taken back by who was at the door.

"Ummm Karma, how did you find out where I live?" He was standing there with two dozen roses and a huge teddy bear. I don't mean like those regular size either; I'm talking about the life like teddy bear.

"Ma, don't insult my intelligence. It's nothing for me to get information, that's here nor there tho. Here, these are for you," he said, passing me the stuff. I took the teddy bear first since it was so big and sat it down, then held the flowers in my hand.

"What is all of this?" I didn't picture Karma being the flower and teddy type of guy.

"I just want to apologize for everything that went on between us yesterday. You're right; there is more to life than just money. You just have to understand where I'm coming from. Growing up, I didn't have shit and I didn't have anyone. The love a parent is supposed to give their child was nonexistent to me. I don't even know who the hell my mother is. Since my own mother didn't love me enough to stay in my life, I figured that love shit was for the birds. When Red put me on, I vowed to put money before everything because money was the only way to make it in this world-"

"No, you don't have to explain," I told him, cutting in.

"I know I don't have to, I want to. Money was the only thing I gave a fuck about until I met you. I'm not saying I'm in love with you or no shit like that. What I'm saying is that you are someone I can see myself falling for. I understand that you been hurt and, in a sense, I been hurt too. We both have things we need to work on and hearts to mend. I'm willing to piece that shit back together if you give me the chance.

I won't lie to you and tell you fuckin' with me will be easy because it probably won't. All I can promise you is that I will give you everything I got, if you give me the same in return. Let me put it this way. I will be the best mistake you ever made or I will change your life; either way, the experience would be one that goes down in history. You don't have to say anything right now because I know everything I just said was a lot. If you willing to fuck with a nigga, send me a text or something."

He leaned in, lightly kissing my cheek, then walked away. There was so much I wanted to say to him, but I was stuck in the moment. I never had no dude do what Karma just did. I closed the front door and went to put my roses in a vase. Karma had basically let me in to see his vulnerable side. I knew he was in the streets and had to remain this hard tough guy, but the dude at my door wasn't that Karma.

I was so at a loss for words I needed to get a second opinion on this. I ran back to my room, grabbing my cell to text Callie and tell her to come over. As I was scrolling through my text messages, I saw Karma's text from this morning and realized I never texted back. Maybe me not texting back was the best thing because instead of a regular conversation, I ended up with a revelation in a sense.

I quickly sent Callie a text, telling her to come over asap. Just as I was about to put the phone down, my phone started ringing. Looking at the caller id, I cursed myself out for not blocking Addison's number.

"Addison, what do you want? I didn't answer your text for a reason."

"The fuck you ignoring me for Royce?"

"I could've sworn that we were broken up. Not to mention, I punched your chick in the nose not too long ago."

"That wasn't my chick; she was just some groupie. You the only chick I got eyes for."

I busted out laughing because this dude was full of shit. "Yeah, me and any other female that is willing to open her legs. Addison, what are you doing on my line?"

"Come on Royce, don't be like that. You know I love you. I just get caught up and shit."

"Am I supposed to just accept the fact that you get caught up and shit. I don't know what type of woman you take me for but I'm not the type that allows a man to continuously walk all over them."

"Nobody isn't walking all over. I slipped up once and I understand that."

"This is why we could never be together because you didn't just slip up once; this is just the only time you got caught. Look, what we had was cool but, obviously, I wasn't who you really wanted. I'm not mad or anything Addison. I just want to really move on. You have your parties to promote and I have my life to live. I wish you nothing but the best," I told him and hung up the phone.

As soon as my phone went back to the home screen, I made sure to block his number. I figured after he tried to call a couple of times and realize he was blocked, he would just leave me alone. I don't know why he was trying to hold on anyway. Now that I think about it, what we had was so high school. We were together, but our relationship lacked real commitment and that was a mistake I wasn't going to make twice. If I decided to get involved with Karma, then I would need reassurance that he was all mine because I would be all his. That cheating shit was something I wasn't going to put up with again. It was gonna have to be all or nothing.

Chapter 12: Callie

"I have to go Trench, but I'll be back later," I told him as I climbed out of bed. We were just about to go another round when Royce texted my phone. She said it was urgent, so I had to leave. Wasn't no dick more important than my best friend.

"Damn, you could've let me get a few more pumps in before you run off, damn."

"You know you not even the few more pumps type of dude. I'll be back later."

"Nah, don't come back cause Karma will be here and he don't like females over here while we supposed to be making that money."

"I thought you were in charge tho?" I questioned, pulling up my jeans.

"It's a partnership but when the time comes, I'ma be the nigga sitting on the crown."

"Uh huh, if I let you tell it. Well, just hit me whenever you're ready to go that other round." Grabbing my bag off the dresser, I left out the room.

"Bye Smitty," I sang, waving.

He hit me with a head nod and I hit him with a seductive smile. Trench was cool and all, but Smitty was everything. Trench wasn't ugly but where he lacked in the looks department, he made up in bed. The only problem with Trench was that he liked to brag about how he was going to be next in line. Shit, I had just met him and I knew he wasn't going to be the next up in line. It was clear as day that Karma was the next to wear the crown. The only reason why I was still fucking with Trench was because the nigga was generous with the money. He didn't have an issue with sharing the wealth.

Some people call me a gold digger, but I don't think the shoe fits. I don't just date men that have money; I only sleep with men who have money. Why would I want to be with a broke nigga that I have to help build up? If a nigga can't get it on his own and needs a woman's help, then the nigga wasn't never shit from the jump. Don't get it twisted. I wasn't just fucking dudes for the money; a couple of them I had feelings for. They weren't deep feelings but feelings nonetheless. The only problem was none of them held my interest for long. It was like, once I got all the money, I no longer saw interest. I guess they were all lame niggas, but Smitty had me wide open.

Dudes with dreads usually didn't attract me but that nigga right there would make me learn how to twist them thangs, so no other chick would play in his hair. Now, me getting a dude's attention was like second nature to me, but Smitty wasn't giving me the time of day. I had seen him around a couple of times but never up close and personal until today. When Trench introduced us, I could've sworn it was love at first sight and that meant something because love wasn't even in my vocabulary.

My only issue was getting Trench off me and figuring out how to get with Smitty. He seemed like the loyal type, so I knew he wouldn't just fuck with me. I was going to have to figure something out because he was too fine to pass up.

I pulled up to Royce mom's house and texted her, letting her know I was outside. It took less than a second to open the door. When she opened it, she damn near dragged my ass inside.

"Damn girl, what you fail your test or something? Pulling on me like you about to beat my ass or some shit."

"For your info, I passed my exam. Wait, were you fucking?" she asked, turning up her nose.

I rolled my eyes and ignored her question. "Well then, what you grabbing on me for?" I went in her fridge, pulled out a can of soda, and sat at the kitchen table.

"So, tell me why Karma showed up at my house with flowers and a teddy bear, basically pouring his heart out to me."

"Get out of here. Karma didn't come over here pouring his heart out and shit. From what Trench says, Karma doesn't do serious relationships."

"Well, Trench is wrong because he came over here letting me know that he wanted to fuck with the kid," she said with a goofy ass grin on her face.

"I know you're happy and everything, but I need you to be careful. Karma may not be at the top, but he is out here getting money and with money comes hoes." It wasn't that I was trying to steal her joy; I just wanted her to know the run down.

"You would know, wouldn't you?" she sassed.

"Don't get an attitude with me because I'm trying to be a friend and keep it real with you. I love you, Royce, like a g and I just don't want to see you hurt again. You just got out of a fucked relationship and I don't want to see you in another one."

"I hear everything you're saying and I appreciate it, but I don't think Karma is going to hurt me and if he does, I doubt it would be intentional. Just like I'm somewhat broken, so is he. We are both taking risks if we choose to be together. So, don't worry me with the negative that may come with our relationship because I'm focused on the positive."

"Then, if you're focused on the positive, so am I. I just want to see you happy, baby girl."

"Enough about me. I see you and Trench have been hanging tough lately. How is that going?"

It's whatever honestly. He's not much to look at, but he got that bomb dick. I just wish I would've met Smitty before I met him."

"Wait, who is Smitty?" she questioned, looking confused.

"Smitty is someone who works for Karma. Bayyybeee, when I say that nigga is fine, he is fine with a capital F. He so fine that he got me wanting to change my ways."

89

"He must be all of that and then some to make you change your ways."

"I just don't think he's going to fuck with me knowing I fucked with Trench."

"Well, maybe you should stop fucking with Trench and give it some time before you step to Smitty."

"Eh, I don't think that's going to work. I'ma figure something out tho because he is too fine to pass up."

"What you need to do right now is go take a shower. Girl, why would you ever come outside after sex and not wash your ass?"

"Excuse me, but someone texted me to come over here asap. To me that means it's an emergency. Stop acting like you never smelt sex before bitch." I laughed.

"Laugh your ass all the way to the shower. You chilling over here for the night?"

"Yeah, I don't have shit else to do."

"Kay. I'll take you out some pajama pants and a t-shirt. We can order Dominos or something."

"Sounds good to me," I told her and went towards her bedroom.

I kicked off my shoes and went into the linen closet, grabbing a towel and wash cloth. I had been over here more times than I can remember, so I knew where everything was. I turned the water on steaming hot, then stripped out of my clothes. Stepping into the shower, I allowed the hot water to rain down on my body.

I honestly did my best thinking when I was in the shower. The only thing on my mind was getting at Smitty. I didn't know what had me so caught up on him, but I felt like he needed to be mine. I guess I could have Royce set up a double date or something. I was going to take Royce's advice and leave Trench alone for now. Hopefully, by the time I stepped to Smitty, all would be forgotten of Trench and I. Shit, even if all wasn't forgotten, I wasn't going to let Trench's ugly ass stop me from getting Smitty. I had my eyes on the prize and a bitch like me always played to win.

Chapter 13: Karma

"The fuck you mean Trench had a chick up in here?"

"Not even on no snitch shit, but that nigga was straight fucking in the back room." I ran my hand over my hair as Smitty gave me the rundown of what happened two days ago.

I was supposed to come back over here after I left Butta's house, but I ended up going back over to Red's spot. I let him know that I made that move towards Butta and when his ass found out, he wanted to celebrate. When I was with Trench yesterday, he didn't say shit about bring Callie over here. I didn't have an issue with Callie; I just wasn't fond of females being in the trap. Shit, I went and got a whole other apartment for shit like that, which was why I didn't understand Trench's reason for fucking her here.

"Ight Smitty, good looking out," I told him.

"You know I got you," he told me, dapping me up.

I left out the apartment and headed towards the front of the projects. There wasn't a day that Mount Haven wasn't on and poppin'. I said wassup to a couple of niggas that I knew and headed for my car. Mount Haven was the type of place where niggas got popped just for lookin'unfamiliar. My hood was wild, but I loved the shit.

As I got in my car, Trench was calling my phone.

"Just the nigga I need to see," I said, answering.

"Wassup?"

"Where you at? We need to meet up and talk about a few things," I told him. "Nah, fuck that, meet me at my crib."

"Ight," he said and I hung up.

I pulled out heading towards Williamsburg. Williamsburg was where I rested my head whenever I wasn't working. I could count on one hand how many people knew about this crib. When it came to where I slept, I was really private. Off the fact that nobody gave a fuck where I was sleeping when I was younger; therefore, they didn't need to give a fuck now. Yeah, a nigga was still holdin' on to his past but that shit was hard to let go. I knew sooner or later, I was gonna have to forgive; today just wasn't that day.

It took all of an hour for me to pull up to my crib. As I was stepping out the car, a text came through on my phone.

Butta:

I want to meet up & talk

I was about to send her a call back when my phone rung. Flashing across the screen was Camellia's name.

"Yo," I answered.

"Eww, why are you answering the phone like that?" she questioned.

"No reason, just what you want?"

"Okay, someone must have pissed in your Cheerios because you have an attitude when I didn't do anything to you."

"My bad ight. I just been stressed lately," I sighed, softening my tone.

"Then why don't you come through and let me ease some of that stress?" her voice was laced with pure seduction.

"Nah, can't do that. I'm a little busy."

"Since when are you too busy to come and blow my back out?"

"Look Camellia, we need to chill out with all of that shit. You a beautiful girl who deserves more than casual sex."

"Uh okay. No problem," she said and hung up the phone.

I thought about calling her back, then quickly changed my mind. She might not have understood where I was coming from now, but she would once she met the dude that was right for her. I was going to make sure to go by her spot to make sure there was no love lost. She still worked for me and I needed her on my team without any drama.

Grabbing a bottle of water, I sat in my living room and turned on the tv. I had a nice two bedroom, one and a half bath condo. It wasn't a mansion but, shit, it was good enough. Flicking through the channels, I decided to watch Everyone Hates Chris until Trench came. I took a sip of my water then grabbed my phone, remembering I had to text Butta back. I said fuck it and, instead of texting, I called her ass.

"Hey," she sang into the phone after the fourth ring.

"Wassup ma, how was your day so far?"

"It's cool; just in the house chilling with my mom before she goes to work."

"Oh ight, sounds cool. What we need to talk about tho?"

"That's a conversation I rather have in person then over the phone."

"Ight, when you want to meet up?"

"We can do something tonight if you want."

"I'm not really in a going out type of mood-"

"What you have to get money or something?" she sassed, cutting me off.

"Chill out Royce. If you would've let me finish you, would've known I was out in Williamsburg. Don't assume shit ight."

"Okay," she said.

For the next couple of minutes, the phone was quiet and the only thing that could be heard was our breathing.

"Yo, you still there?" I asked.

"Yeah, I'm here."

"Come through and we can have dinner and watch a movie."

"Are you cooking?"

"If you liked burnt food, then I got you," I joked.

"On second thought, I'll do the cooking. Just let me know when you're ready for me to come over."

"You can come over like around six. I'll text you the address. Butta, I got to go," I told her as I made my way to the front door. Opening the door, I dapped up Trench and stepped to the side, allowing him in.

"Uh okay. I'll see you when I get there."

"Ight Butta," I told her and hung up.

"Nigga, let me find out Butta got you boo lovin' and shit on the phone," Trench joked, but I didn't find shit funny.

"Don't worry about what she got me doin'. What you need to be worrying about is why you thought it was cool for you to bring Callie to the spot where we keep our money, just to fuck. You could've brought her to the other spot my nigga."

"The fuck you buggin' for and going off on me like I'm some kind of bitch?"

"Nigga, that move you pulled shows that you are a bitch."

"You over here about to bust a blood vessel over some shit that's not even that deep. Yeah, I fucked Callie at the spot; so fuckin' what. You act like you not messin' with her best friend and shit."

"Nigga, you using that as an excuse." I laughed. Trench was really trying to sell me some bullshit as if I was some stupid nigga.

"Nah, it's not an excuse because I don't make those. I'm telling you what it is. I don't know why Smitty ass is dry snitchin' and shit."

"This shit isn't about Smitty; it's about you thinking you can do as you fuckin' please. I don't give a fuck who the bitch is that you fucked; the whole point is you brought the bitch to our spot. The fuck you think I'm paying rent on that other apartment for?"

"You actin' like Callie is on some treacherous type of shit."

"You don't know what the fuck she on because you don't even know the bitch. Look, this going back and forth shit is for the birds. Don't bring no fuckin' body to that spot ight."

"Hol' the fuck up! Why you talkin' to me like you my boss or some shit? I run Mount Haven just like you do, nigga. I don't stand behind you; I stand right next to yo ass. Therefore, I can bring whichever bitch I want to that spot."

"Nigga, you steady trying to turn this shit into a power struggle when it's not even about that."

"You claim that it's not about that but that's what I'm getting out of this whole conversation."

"You over here wildin' on the real. You already heard what I said; don't bring no bitches to the spot and it's just that simple," I told him.

He was standing there ice grilling me like that was supposed to put fear in my heart. Trench should've know better than anyone, no man on this earth intimidated me.

"The fuck you standing there like you gonna pop off or something? If you got some ill feelings, then speak that shit because if not, get the fuck out my house nigga."

"You got it," he said, nodding his head then heading for the door.

In all the years that I worked with Trench, the nigga never tried to boss up until today. I don't know if he ate his Wheaties or something this morning, but the nigga needed to fall in line. He and I both knew that I was the head nigga in charge at Mount Haven. Trench was my man, so I wasn't going to pull rank but if he ever tried to step to me on some power type of bullshit, I was gonna have to handle him accordingly.

Chapter 14: Royce

"Where you jumping up to run off too?" my mother questioned.

"Umm, I sorta kind of have a date." I smiled.

"Oh and just who is this young man that you have a date with?"

"His name is Karma."

"That's an interesting name."

"It's an interesting name for an interesting guy mom."

"Mhm. Well, it's good to see that you got over your break-up so fast."

Something about what she said had me a little uneasy. I turned around, so that I was facing her. "I'm not over my break- up; I'm just choosing not to dwell in it. It hurts knowing that the man I loved for the past six years didn't love me enough to keep his dick in his pants. My heart is crushed behind Addison, but how long am I supposed to wallow in my sorrow? In order for my heart to mend, I have to go out and live. So, that's exactly what I'm doing. I'm simply living life with no limits."

"I don't want you to take what I said the wrong way. I'm happy you are going out and having fun, instead of staying in and crying over that no good boy. I just don't want you to get caught up again."

"I'm not going to get caught up again because I'm not putting up with the same things I used too. Ma, when I tell you I listened to everything you told me about men, I'm serious. As a woman, I know my worth and I refuse to let any man treat me as if he doesn't know my worth too."

"That's my baby girl. All I want is for you to be truly happy."

"That's all I want too. I'm not saying Karma and I going to get married tomorrow, but he seems cool. What's going to make things easy with us is that we both know the other person has things to work on; therefore, there won't be no high expectations that neither one of us can't reach."

"Alright now Royce. I'ma stop talking to you about this because you sounding like you about to teach me a thing or two." My mother laughed.

"I could never teach you anything because everything I know is because of you."

"I love you, Royce."

"I love you too, ma."

I rushed over to my mother on the bed and hugged her nice and tight. I was really appreciative of my mother. Yes, she was my mother but she was also my best friend. I could tell her any and everything without any judgment. Of course, she would tell me when she disapproved of my actions, but she would also make sure that I was taught a lesson in the situation. My mother was truly a beautiful woman and if I could be half the woman that she is at her age, I would be more than happy. My mother was simply a beautiful woman through and through.

∞ ∞ ∞

As the cab pulled up to the address Karma gave me, my hands began to sweat and my heart started racing two times its normal speed.

"Calm down Royce. You have been alone with him before. Relax," I told myself out loud.

"Miss, are you okay?" the cabbie asked me. He was giving me a strange look from rearview mirror.

"Uh yeah, I'm fine. How much is it?"

"Sixty-five dollars."

"Damn," I whispered. I pulled out the money, handed it to him, then sent Karma a quick text before stepping out the cab. I ran my hands over my olive green dress, trying to smooth it out. The longer I stood there waiting for Karma, the more my nerves started to get the best of me.

"I'm out of here," I sighed, turning and heading back out to the street.

"Butta, where you think you goin'?"

His deep raspy voice stopped me in my tracks. I slowly turned around on my heels. As soon as our eyes connected, a smile spread across my face. I was smiling hard as hell because my cheeks began to slightly hurt. I slowly made my way to him, trying to calm myself down in my head.

"Where were you trying to go?" he asked, once I reached him at the front of his building.

"Uh, nowhere. I thought I dropped something and the wind blew it away," I lied.

"Butta, you don't have to lie to me. If you were having second thoughts 'bout chilling with me, then it's cool."

"I wouldn't say I had second thoughts; I just got nervous that's all."

"There's no need to be nervous. We just chilling lil mama." He smiled, grabbing my hand.

Leading me into the building, we went up to the top floor. We walked in his house and it was breathtaking. Walking in, you had to walk down a long hallway before you reached the living room. In the hallway, there were pictures of 2pac, Biggie, Nas, and, of course, Jay Z. What set the hallway off was the black and white color scheme he had going on. Once you hit the living room, the color scheme went from white and black to black and navy blue. The walls were navy blue while his furniture was black leather. I was amazed that a guy would have such good taste.

"Come on, let me give you a quick tour." He smiled, tugging my hand.

"Okay." I cheesed. I didn't know what it was, but he had me smiling my ass off for no reason at all.

He showed me the rest of the house and I fell in love with each room. Every room had a different color scheme, which portrayed a different personality so it seemed. His kitchen was gold and black, which was different but pretty, nonetheless. His bedroom was what stood out the most to me. His bedroom was olive green, black, and gold. I would've never pictured those three colors together but it worked. His bedroom furniture looked like black glass with hints of gold, while everything else was olive green.

"So wassup, tell me what you thinking?"

"Your house is beautiful. I didn't think a dude like you would have such good style," I jocked, slightly bumping into him.

"Damn, you not holdin' back huh?" He chuckled. "I like the simple things that are still the finer things in life."

"So complex, yet still so simple." I smiled.

"Yeah, something like that." He pulled me to him and wrapped his arms directly above my butt. I wouldn't even say my body tensed up because it was worse than that. It was like my body was frozen. I was stiff as hell in his arms; I guess he could tell because he started laughing.

"Damn Butta, I have that type of effect on you?"

"No," I sassed.

"Relax, Royce, all I'm doing is holdin' you; now, if I was to grip ya ass, then you would have a problem." He gripped my ass, causing me to jump a little. I punched him in his chest and placed my hands on my hips.

"Karma, that is off limits."

"Butta, you got a mean little punch. I'ma need you to watch them hands tho."

"You watch yours and I'll watch mine."

"On the sly, I don't wanna watch my hands." Karma smoothly rubbed his hands while hitting me with his infamous smirk that showed off his dimples.

"Before you try to rub your hands like bird man, you should make sure them thangs have lotion on them."

"Shots fired." He laughed.

"Just keeping it real." I shrugged.

"That's all I ever want you you to do." He pulled me back into him and, this time, my body was more relaxed.

"Wassup, you said you wanted to talk to me about something."

"Uh yeah, I... umm... I want to explore whatever this is between us," I shyly said.

"Nah, don't turn ya head. You wanna rock with a nigga, then you need to look me in the eye while you say it. When someone can't look you in the eye, it's because they have something to hide. What you got to hide Royce?" The way his mouth formed my name had me wondering how it would feel to have his mouth on my spot. The two had nothing to do with each other but, somehow, they seemed so good together.

"I don't have nothing to hide," I told him. I made sure to stare at him intensely in his eyes, so he would know what I was saying was true.

"Yeah ight, then tell me what needs to be said." He cupped my chin, bringing my face closer to his. We were so close that I could feel his cool breath against my lips, I would even take it as far as saying I could slightly taste the winter fresh gum he was chewing whenever I licked my lips.

"I want to see what's this connection the two of us have."

"Oh, we have a connection Butta." He hit me with that pretty boy smile of his, almost making my knees buckle.

"You know we have a connection, so I don't even know why you're questioning it. I got you doing things you don't normally do. So, that can only mean one thing."

"Oh really and what one thing is that?"

I leaned in closer, matching my lips perfectly to his. "It means that I got you whipped without giving you any of my sweet stuff," I said against his lips.

"That's where you got me fucked up." He scooped me up, then gently placed me on the bed. He laid on top of me, pinning my arms above my head. All that brave shit I was feeling a little while ago was now gone. My heart was beating fast and the words I thought to say in my head just wouldn't make it to my vocal cords.

"You don't got me whipped Butta, so don't ever think that. Being whipped is something that little boys deal with and there ain't shit little about me. I'm a man, which is why I stepped to you the way I did."

"O… o… ok," I whispered.

"Now, you can chill out and make yourself at home or you can go in the kitchen and start cookin' whatever it is that you makin'. I have to handle something right fast, so I'ma be in my office. Give me like an hour or so to get some shit straight, then you got my undivided attention."

"Uh okay."

"Don't go searching through my shit either Butta," he said, walking towards the door.

"You don't have to worry about me searching through your stuff. You don't belong to me."

Instead of Karma saying anything, he licked his lips and smirked, showing off those dimples. I blushed a little as he climbed off of me. He looked at me before he walked out of his room and I stuck my middle finger up at him. Of course, he laughed, paying my ass no mind, then left out the room. I waited a couple of seconds before rushing to his drawers. I know I had no right searching his things, but I couldn't help it. If it's one thing I knew, it was when a female fucked with a dude, she usually left something behind. Karma hadn't said anything about being involved with anyone, but I wasn't stupid. He was handsome and had money, both those things attracted bitches.

I looked all through his drawers but found nothing. My search went from the bedroom to the living room and even the guest room. I was glad that I didn't find anything, but I was still going to ask him about any female that he was fuckin' with. With Addison, I never questioned him about anything because I didn't want him thinking I was trying to keep tabs on him or anything. With Karma, I wanted things to be different. I wanted us to have a more open relationship, especially with the line of work that he was in.

Going into his kitchen, I looked around, seeing what I could cook. There was a bag on the counter that caught my attention. Going through it, I saw it was some stuffed salmon and shrimp. I laughed a little because Karma already knew what he wanted to eat. I figured I could whip up some shrimp scampi with the stuff salmon and broccoli on the side. I opened every cabinet and every draw looking for everything I would need. Once I had everything on the counter, I started getting to work.

His kitchen was beautiful, mainly due to the fact that it looked as though it had never been touched. All the appliances were state of the art. I danced around the kitchen as I cooked to the music that was playing from my galaxy S4.

"Mhmm, it smell good as fuck in here," I heard Karma say.

"That's because you are so used to bringing chicks into your bedroom; you never give them a chance to show you if they can cook or not," I told him. I took a quick look at him over my shoulder and winked.

"I don't bring girls to where I lay my head because none of them are important. If we fuckin', then we gettin' a room."

"You don't even fuck girls at that other apartment?"

"Nah, I don't like to mix business with pleasure. When I'm over there, it's because I'm getting money. I don't need to be eleven inches deep in some pussy, then gotta be called away to body a nigga."

"So, why would you bring me there to chill then?"

"Chillin' and fuckin' are two different things. I don't mind chillin' with a female there because it's nothing to just get up and leave. Bein' in some pussy and havin' to stop is the hardest shit on a nigga."

"Oh, I guess. Dinner will be done soon," I told him, ready to change the whole direction of this conversation. Karma talking about having relations with other girls caused me to feel slightly jealous.

"Ight, that's cool. You want me to go find a movie or some shit?"

"If you want."

"Nah, it's not about what I want; it's all about you, Butta. If you want me to stay in here and keep you company, then that's what I'll do."

"Then yeah, I guess you can stay."

"Ight then and why was you going through my stuff?"

"I was just making myself at home. Isn't that what you said to do?" I said, playing it cool.

"Yeah ight, yo ass was searching for something. What was you looking for?"

"How did you even know I was searching?" I answered his question with a question because I was trying to figure out if I could tell him the truth without looking crazy.

"Just because I'm not at the top of the food chain doesn't mean I don't have niggas trying to end me."

"So, you have cameras?"

"Yeah and the monitor in my office, which doubles as a panic room. Now, what were you looking for?"

"I was looking for any traces of a woman being here."

"Really." He laughed. I rolled my eyes at him, then went to grab some plates because the food was now done.

"You could've just asked me some shit like that. When it comes to you, I'm an open book."

I nodded my head, letting him know I heard him but didn't say anything. I fixed both of our plates and brought them to the table. Before I could sit down, Karma got up to pull out my chair. I blushed a little because the gesture was cute. He then went in the fridge, pulling out two sodas and two bottles of water. He sat them in between our plates, then sat across from me.

"Why didn't you ask me if I was fucking with any other chicks?" his question broke our silence.

"I don't know, but I'm asking now. Is there any chick out there that might be mad at the fact we dating?"

"Truth, Camellia is a chick I used to fuck whenever I was stressed. I wasn't playing her or leaving her to believe we were in a relationship. We had a mutual understanding, so everything is cool. Will I have to be in contact with her? Yes because she works for me. She keeps all my baggers and cookers in line and she's the best at what she does."

"Okay." I stuffed a piece of fish in my mouth, trying to gather my thoughts. I didn't want to tell him that he had to fire ole girl, but I wasn't happy with the fact he would still be in contact with her.

"Look, I already know what you thinkin' and you don't got shit to worry about. Anything that goes on between Camellia and I is straight business from this point on. I'm not in the business of hurting you, Royce, and I mean that shit."

"I trust you," I told him.

"That's all that I ask. I already told you things may not be easy, but I would never do anything intentional to hurt you or cause you any pain."

"I know."

He reached out and placed his hand across the table. I placed mines in his and a shock of energy went through my body. I wasn't exactly sure what it was but, for me, it was confirmation on what I was doing. It was confirmation that seeing where things could go between us was the right thing to do.

"You better eat your food before it gets cold," I told him.

"Trust me, this food not getting cold; it's hot as hell," he joked.

"You so silly." I laughed.

We made idle talk while we ate and it was cool. We laughed, smiled, and just enjoyed each other's company. When we were done, I cleaned up the kitchen, then found him in the living room searching through On-Demand.

"Is there anything particular you wanna watch?" he asked me.

"Not really, I watch just about anything." I shrugged.

"Ight cool. There's this show on Netflix I been trying to catch up on called The 100. I heard it's supposed to be good."

"Okay, we can watch it."

He went to Netflix and when I saw what type of show it was, I turned towards Karma with a skeptical look on my face.

"You watch this kind of show?" I asked him.

"Yeah. Just because I'm a thug doesn't mean I don't like sy-fy and shit. If there was ever a zombie apocalypse or the world was going to end, I'm the nigga you would want to have around."

"I guess it's a good thing I'm callin' you mine now, huh?"

"I guess so Butta." The way he was looking at me wasn't sexual; it was more so affectionate. I blushed under his gaze, mostly because of the inappropriate thoughts I was having. I wanted Kama in the worse way.

"Whenever you ready to give in to temptation, let me know." He smiled, then turned his attention back to the tv.

Was I that easy to read? I questioned myself. I needed to pull myself together and quick. The show came on and it seemed interesting. I got comfortable, moving a little bit closer to Karma. When he saw I was trying to get closer, he simply scooped me up and laid me across his lap. His hand rested on my waist as we both watched the tv. The first episode flew by and I was more than ready for the next.

"That shit was good huh?" he asked.

"Yeah, it was. Don't start the next episode; I have to pee right quick."

"Ight, hurry up tho before you be assed out."

"Boy, you better not play with me. I'll be right back."

I jumped off the couch and rushed to the bathroom. I peed, washed my hands, and was ready to get back to the show. As I got closer to the living room, I heard him laughing. It wasn't a normal laugh though; it was dark and kind or tormented. I eased my way into the living and notice he had my phone in his hand.

"Nigga, make this the last time you call this phone ight. I'm not about all this talkin' shit. I bust my nines and bodies fall. Fuck with me if you want to nigga." He hung the phone up, then tossed it at me.

"You ready?" he questioned, like he just wasn't threating someone on my phone.

"Who were you talking to?"

"It don't even matter. The only nigga you should be concerned with is right here. Come on, so we can finish watching this show."

I sat down and cuddled back up against him. I assumed Addison was the person who was on the phone. I had no clue how he called when I blocked his number. I wanted to ask Karma was he really going to kill Addison if he kept calling my phone. Something told me that was the wrong thing to question. I just really hoped Addison took Karma's threat seriously and stayed away. I still loved him, but I was no longer in love with him. That didn't mean I wanted to see him dead though.

Chapter 15: Callie

"Just like that Cal, work that ass ma." Trench slapped my ass as my hips worked him

I bucked and bounced, giving him all I had to offer. I thought it was the least I could do since I was ending things with him. I wanted to end things with him sooner, but his dick game was too bomb to walk away from. Now, here we were a month and a half later, and I was now ready to end things.

"FUCK CALLIE!" he groaned. His grip on my hips was tight as hell as he held me in place. The way he was whimpering; if he didn't have this condom on, I would be pregnant for sure.

When he was done cumming. I slid off of him and headed straight for the bathroom to clean myself up. After I told him we were done, I wanted to exit stage left as fast as possible. I kind of felt bad for how I was treating him but, shit, the heart wanted what the heart wanted. Smitty was still on my radar and the sooner I got rid of Trench, I would be able to make my move on him. Whenever I saw Smitty, I was always with Trench, which was fucking up my game. I didn't want to seem like a hoe because that wasn't me. I just so happened to meet the wrong dude and now I was trying to make corrections.

"What you doin' in the bathroom? You don't want to cuddle or do whatever it is that you chicks like to do after sex?" Trench asked.

"Give me a couple of minutes and I'll be right out," I called back out to him.

I rushed to clean myself up because I wanted to make this as quick as possible. I counted to five, trying to get my words together. Once I felt I had a pretty good idea of what I was going to say, I opened the bathroom door.

"Damn, took you long enough," he said from the bed.

"Yeah, well I didn't want to leave out smelling like sex," I told him.

My clothes were scattered all over the bedroom, which didn't make my escape any easier. I slipped on my panties and bra, then went for my jeans and shirt.

"Why you getting dressed; where you going? I thought we were chilling for the day?"

"About that... I don't think we should see each other anymore. It's been fun, but I don't think this is what I see in my future."

"The fuck you mean this isn't what you see in your future?"

"Trench, I can't put it any clearer than it already is. I don't want to end whatever it is that we have going on. I been with you for a month and I still don't know where you rest your head or anything about you. All we do is come to these random hotels to fuck each other's brains out."

"Callie, you trippin' for real ma. The fuck you need to know where I rest my head at. You plan on killing a nigga or settin' me up?"

"No, stupid. How am I supposed to know you are serious about us when I don't even know you? We been messing around for a month and a fuckin' half Trench and I know nothing about you other than your age and what you do for a living."

"In my eyes, that's all you need to know."

"And that's fine because that's how you feel. I feel like this is a dead end street and I'm tired of driving on it." I slipped my feet into my flip flops and snatched up my bag. For the most part, the conversation was going fine and, for a second, I thought I was going to just walk out without any issues. Trench had other plans.

"Nah, chill the fuck out Callie because yo ass ain't going nowhere. If you were feeling some type of way, all you had to do was talk to a nigga."

"I didn't feel the need to talk to you because what we had isn't even anything serious. We can still be cool; I just don't want to fuck with you like that."

"The fuck you gonna do without me huh, Callie? You think any other nigga that's makin' that bread is going to fuck with you after I done been all in them guts? I'm your best fuckin' bet at going to the top, so I advise you to sit yo ass down and order some room service or something."

"Trench, what are you talkin' about?"

"You think I don't know what type of chick you are? Bitch, I knew about you before I even got with yo gold digger ass. The only reason I fucked with you is because I thought we could help each other out. I needed a bad bitch on my arm and you needed money."

"So, you were just using me?" I asked shocked. I don't know why I was shocked but I was. Trench was showing me a side of him I never saw before.

"Wasn't you just using me? It hurts when the tables are turned huh." He laughed. I took off my shoe and threw it at his ass, hitting him in the head.

"You fuckin' bitch!" he yelled, getting off the bed.

I snatched the door open and rushed out. This nigga was so caught up in chasing me, he didn't realize he ran out the room ass naked. I ran past an old white lady just as she was saying oh my and staring at Trench. I jetted towards the elevator and pressed the button, getting on. I let out a sigh of relief, happy as hell that Trench had to stop the chase because he was naked. The conversation didn't go as smoothly as I would've hoped, but I was happy it was finally over. Now, I had free reign to holla at Smitty.

I don't care what no one said; Smitty was made for me. Everything about him complimented everything about me. The few times I'd been around him had me feeling him even more. He was funny, smart, and driven. To me, he was my equal and I knew when we got together, there wasn't nothing that we wouldn't be able to accomplish.

117

The elevator came to the lobby and I stepped off with only one shoe on. Everyone was staring at me, but I walked right out that bitch with my head held high. I couldn't have been anymore happier when I made it to my car. It was seven at night and I knew Karma was out handling business, leaving Royce with nothing really to do.

I was in a celebrating mood and since she was my only friend, I needed her to be in one too. I set my phone up to my car system and pulled off, just as Royce's number was being dialed.

"I was starting to think that you fell in love with Trench or something."

"Ew, why would you ever say that?" I asked her.

"You didn't have to be so harsh and because it seems like you are always with him." I giggled a little because Royce really believed that I stayed underneath Trench, when in reality, I would be out following Smitty around. Yeah, a bitch was obsessed and shit but so what? In my mind, Smitty was mine, so it really wasn't stalking.

"Just because I enjoy the company of his penis doesn't mean I enjoy his company. None of that really matter's anymore anyway because I ended things with him."

"Why would you do that?"

"Because whatever we had going on wasn't going anywhere. Yes, I got a good orgasm but it was time wasted. Orgasms can come a dime a dozen but time, you can't get back. I rather give someone my time who deserves it and Trench wasn't worthy."

"Well, if you say so. I thought the two of you were cute."

"We may have been cute but the situation wasn't. Anyway, what you doing?" I asked, changing the conversation real fast. I tried explaining the Smitty thing to Royce multiple times, but she just didn't get it.

"Nothing, just came back from dropping my mom off at work. Her car started over smoking when she was leaving, so I just dropped her off," Royce explained.

"Must be nice to have a dude that lets you drive around in his car."

"It's not even like that. I was willing to buy my own, but Karma wants me to save my money."

"You see, that's the type of nigga that I need in my life."

"You had that type of nigga in Trench."

"Uh no, I didn't. That type of nigga is Smitty and now that Trench and I are over, I need you to make that introduction."

"Why do I need to introduce the two of you when y'all know each other?" I sighed because sometimes Royce could be so dumb.

"He knows the Callie that was fuckin' with his boy; he needs to know the newly single and available Callie."

"If you say so. I'm supposed to be meetin' Karma over there later tonight to pick him up. You can come with me; I don't want to be driving over there on my own anyway."

"Oh perfect and we can all go out to the club or something afterwards."

"I don't know about all that, but I'll see. You can meet me at my mom's house around ten."

"Okay, you want me to drive or you want me to ride with you?"

"It's on you. I know Karma will be driving back, so it's your call."

"I'll ride with you."

"Okay, I'll see you then."

"Okay."

Hanging up the phone, a smile crept on my face. Now, any other person would've drove to meet Royce, so they wouldn't have to be a third wheel on the way back. Me, on the other hand, I was gonna ride with her so hopefully Smitty would have to drop me off. I had the perfect plan; now, I just needed everything to go accordingly.

As I was thinking about my night ahead of me, I noticed my tank was almost on E. I pulled into the Hess gas station that was to my left. Stepping out of my car, my eyes just so happened to fall upon my soul mate. Me running into Smitty at the gas station was fate. No, fate wasn't even a strong enough word; it was more so like destiny. I casually, yet seductively, walked over to where Smitty was pumping his gas.

"Um hey, do you mind helping me pump my gas?" I asked, as if I didn't recognize him.

"Yeah, I got you Callie; why you actin' like you don't know me and shit?" He smiled cockily. Being up close and personal with him had me stuck. Those pretty light brown eyes of his had me falling in love.

"Oh shit Smitty, I didn't even realize that was you." I giggled, playing it off.

"Yeah ight. Where ya boy at?" he asked, looking around.

"You would know better than me. I don't mess with him."

"Oh word damn. When that shit happen?" The way he was inquiring into Trench and I's relationship led me to believe he was interested in me, which had me hype as hell.

"We stopped talking a few weeks back."

"That sucks; the two of you looked good together," he said, finishing up pumping his gas.

"Just cause we looked good together doesn't mean we were good together."

"Yeah, you right. I know all about that shit. Where ya car at?"

"Pump five. I'ma go put the money on it now."

I strutted towards the store and put a little something extra in my walk. I was so busy trying to hypnotize Smitty with my walk that I didn't notice the crack in the cement. My ass ended up tripping and stumbling a little. I looked back to see if Smitty saw what happened. Our eyes locked while he laughed. I rolled my eyes at him and continued to strut, as if that little stumble never even happened. I was embarrassed as hell, but I wasn't going to let Smitty know it. As I was walking in, some bitch was walking out.

"If you wasn't trying to show off something you don't have, you never would've tripped," she had the nerve to say.

"Hoe, mind your own fuckin' business. I don't even know your ugly ass."

The girl just laughed and continued walking. My high of seeing Smitty was blown, so I was more than ready to go.

"Thirty dollars on pump five please," I told the cashier.

Passing him the money, I walked out going over to my car.

"Smitty, who the hell are you over here pumping gas for?" I heard someone yell. Hearing the name Smitty coming out of a female's mouth caught my attention real quick. Looking towards my car, I saw it was the chick who had something smart to say about me stumbling.

"Umm, is there a problem?" I smirked, walking up to Smitty and leaning on his shoulder.

"Smitty, who the fuck is this hoe because I'm about to introduce her face to brass knuckles," he chick said going through her purse.

"Chill the fuck out Mimi because it's not even that fucking serious. She fucks with Trench. I'm just helping her out," Smitty explained.

"Nigga, you just going to stand here and lie to my face. I know you seen the way this hoe was trying to switch her nonexistent ass."

"The fuck was you watching me so hard. I don't play with cats, so you need to move along. Smitty, thanks for pumping my gas but next time, keep your mutts in line. I don't know what she heard, but you need to let her ass know I don't scare easily. You may play with brace knuckles, but I play with them thangs that could end you in a second. Now, if you don't mind, get the fuck away from my car before my niceness runs out."

I strutted to the other side of my car and got inside. I waited a couple of seconds to see if this bitch was gonna do anything stupid, so I could run her ass over. Smitty ended up having to pull her away because she was on some rah rah shit. I pulled off extra fast, making sure to make that screeching noise. The noise was just for a more dramatic effect on my exit. I was kicking myself for not realizing Smitty was fucking with someone. It was cool because I saw no competition. There was no ring on her finger, which meant Smitty was fair game, and even if there was a ring, that shit wouldn't mean shit.

I wish that bitch didn't have on glasses and that ugly ass sun hat, so I could get a good look at her face. One thing these bitches in New York were good for was running up on a bitch when she least expected it. If she did run up, then that would be her mistake, not mine. I lied about having a gun but what I did have was these hands and these hands worked real good.

I still had every intention of going with Royce to pick up Karma. This little incident that happened did nothing but fuel my fire for Smitty even more. The way I saw it, that bitch was just an obstacle that was gonna have to get knocked down.

Chapter 16: Karma

"You know that bitch had the nerve to end things with me like I'm some chop type of nigga," Trench stressed. The nigga had been talking about Callie for the past three hours. The nigga walked in talking shit about her and he was still going.

"Why don't you just admit that you hurt she ended things?"

"I'm not hurt, fuck that bitch. When a nigga get to the top, she better not bring her hoe ass back over here unless she supply the whole team with that sloppy toppy. Bitch got nerve to say how was she supposed to know I was into her if I didn't tell her shit about me or bring her to my crib. That bitch sounded like a straight ops, on some real shit. You better make sure Royce is true blue. You know that saying, birds of a feather flock together. Shit, Callie lookin' real suspect in my eyes."

"Just because Callie fucked you up, don't bring Royce into this shit. My bitch is as thorough as it gets."

"Ight nigga, damn, I was just saying. Shit. As soon as I talk about Royce, this nigga wanna jump down my throat and shit. Smitty, you see this love struck nigga," Trench joked. I didn't find shit funny though. Butta was something that I didn't play with when it came to other niggas.

"Nah, you were dead wrong for what you said. How would you feel if someone put ya shawty name in the same sentence as some negative shit? You basically said Royce is the ops."

"The fuck got y'all so uptight and shit? I was just expressing how I feel and shit. Now, if shawty really is an ops and I didn't tell y'all what the fuck her best friend said, you would be pissed the fuck off. So, excuse me for relaying a fucking message. Next time, I know to keep my mouth shut."

"Nigga, did Callie say she was the ops or are you assuming shit?" I barked.

"Yo, what the fuck got your panties in a bunch? I wasn't even going to say nothing but since you trying to punk me and shit, you been acting real bitch like since you started fucking with her. She got your head all messed up. How you over here questioning your nigga and shit? I been with you since we were fifteen and hugging the block, and this how you treat a nigga? You don't have to worry; it's all love on my end."

"Ight, both of y'all taking this shit too far. Trench, you know you were dead wrong for accusing Royce of that shit. She is gone off of Karma, not to mention that ain't even the type of person she is. Karma, you can't get mad because this nigga was voicing his opinion. Yeah, he could've said it differently, but I doubt the shit was malicious."

I looked at Smitty, then back at Trench. Right before I could say anything, I heard Royce say the code word. Smitty went to open the door, but I stopped him. I pulled out my nine and swung the door open, pointing it at the person who made me the happiest in the world.

"Karma wha... wha... what are you doing?" she asked, panicked. Her, along with Callie's, hands were up in the air.

"Come in and don't say shit," I told them.

They eased into the apartment with the look of fear and confusion. I know Royce was trying to figure out what the hell was going on because literally twenty minutes ago, we were texting and everything was all good.

"Royce, you fuckin' with them pigs?" I asked calmly. This was the type of shit that kept me from fuckin' with females. In my line of business, I didn't have time for fuck ups. I can't even lie, having this gun pointed at Butta was breaking my heart. Butta was a woman that I could potentially fall in love with, but business had to come first. If Royce was setting me up and I didn't know because I was blinded by love, that shit would make me feel like less of man.

"Karma, what the hell are you talkin' about? Royce isn't no fuckin' snitch!" Callie yelled.

"Callie, shut the fuck up ight," I told her. I was still staring Royce in the eyes as she looked back into mine. The fear and confusion that was once in her eyes disappeared.

"Karma, you got a lot of fuckin' nerve pointing that gun at me. You really think that I'm the type of person that would set you up?" she questioned, moving closer to me. I lowered my gun and tossed it to Smitty.

"I don't know what type of chicks you are used to messing with but not everyone is out to do you fucking dirty," she spat, raising her hand.

She went to swing, but I caught it and twisted her arm behind her back. "Chill the fuck out," I told her.

"No Karma, you get the fuck off of me. How dare you point a fucking gun in my face. A gun, Karma!" she yelled. "Callie, get this nigga off of me now!"

Callie went to move towards me until I stared at her, letting her know if she came this way her ass was getting fucked up.

"Callie, mind your fuckin' business."

"Callie, don't fucking listen to his dumb ass; get him the fuck off of me, so I can go."

"Royce, shut the fuck up because your ass isn't going anywhere until I say so. Matter of fact, y'all niggas hold this down right quick; I'll be back."

I let go of Royce's arm, scooped her short ass up, and threw her over my shoulder. I left out the apartment and made my away to the spare apartment, all the while Royce screamed and punched my back. When we got to the other apartment, I quickly dropped her on the floor.

"You could've sat me back down on my feet," she sassed, rubbing her butt.

"Chill out with all that punching and shit. I already told you about watching them hands."

"You got nerve telling me to watch my hands. Aren't you the same asshole that had a gun to my face."

"My bad about that shit," I apologized.

"That's all you have to fucking say is my bad. You know what? I don't even know why I'm doing this shit. Karma, lose my fucking number," she spat.

She went for the front door and I quickly stood in front of it. "Move the hell out of my way. I don't have anything else to say to your lame ass."

"Oh, so I'm lame now Butta?"

"You been fucking lame." This whole thing was comical because swearing wasn't something Butta did often.

"Then, why you fucking with a nigga then?"

"It doesn't even matter because I'm not fucking with you like that."

"Yeah ight," I told her.

She was standing in front of me with her arms crossed over her ample titties. She was wearing a pair of tight ass spandex looking shorts that had her ass on swole. On top, she was rockin' a cute little bedazzled looking bra with a suit vest covering her. I allowed my eyes to travel down her legs and to her feet. The ankle boots she had on had her legs looking never ending.

Butta was looking good as fuck. Butta never said she had a rule on how long we had to wait to have sex, so I decided to give it some time. Looking at her right now, though, proved to me that she had all the time in the world. A nigga was backed up and eager to roam her body.

"I don't know why you looking at me like that because you definitely ain't getting none of this."

"You don't even believe that shit you just said."

"I don't have to believe because it's the truth. Now if you don't mind, move out of my way." I stepped to the side, allowing her room to walk closer to the door.

Once she was close enough, I pushed her up against it with her back to my chest. Her breathing got heavy as she tried to slow it down.

"Relax." I caressed her hips all the way to her breasts.

I gently tugged on her nipples, causing them to get erect in seconds. A soft seductive moan escaped her lips as I slowly and tenderly groped her chest. I took each of her hands into one of my mine, raising them above her head. I used my right foot to kick her legs apart.

"Don't fuckin' move until I tell you to," I told her.

I stepped away from her and went into the fridge, grabbing a can of whip cream. I stripped out of my clothes and made my way back to Royce. Leaning my naked body against hers, I reached around her, dropping her shorts around her ankles.

"The fuck you comin' outside with no panties on for?" I asked, yanking her head back by her hair.

"You could see my pantie line through my shorts. It would've killed my outfit," she explained.

"Then, you shouldn't have worn the fucking shorts or yo ass could've put on a thong or some shit." I let her hair go but pushed her closer to the door. I reached around her, gracing her clit with the presence of my fingers.

"Royce, don't fuckin' play with me ight. I don't play that no panties shit," I roughly told her.

My finger was running laps around her clit as her legs shake. She arched her back, giving me full access to her spot. I rubbed a little faster, tugging on her clit every other lap.

"AHHHH Karma!" she moaned.

"I don't want you saying shit unless it's the words 'I'm cuming'." I smacked her ass hard, so she knew I wasn't playing.

The more I rubbed, the more her body gave into me. She was panting but wasn't one word comin' out her mouth. I slipped two fingers in her while my pinky finger danced around her asshole.

"Karma, I'm cumming," she sang and that shit was like music to my ears. Her pussy muscles gripped my fingers as she released her juices. Slipping my finger out, I ran it across her lips before she took it into her mouth. Butta's tongue glided all around my fingers as she sucked and slurped. That shit was sexy as hell. I rubbed all on her ass while she sucked my fingers. My eyes closed as I enjoyed the feeling.

"Lay across the couch," she whispered, easing my fingers out her mouth. She seductively spun around and dropped her vest by the door. I smirked and laid across the couch. She took long, sexy strides towards me. The way she would cross her foot over the other one in those heels did something to me. The sight was sexy as fuck. When she got close to me, she unsnapped her bra, freeing my two new best friends. She straddled me with her back towards my face.

"Lift up a little." She did as she was told and I sprayed some whip cream all over her pearl.

"That's cold Karma." She giggled.

I leaned over, sitting the can on the coffee table, then forced her on to my face. I feasted on her kitty. The mixture of her juices and whip cream had me feenin' for more.

"Yessssss," she hissed.

"What the fuck I tell you? Don't say shit unless its-"

"I'm cumming!!!" she cooed.

"That's my girl," I smirked. Spreading her ass cheeks, I dived in, making sure it caught it all. Butta's juices was my favorite drink and I wasn't about to waste a drop.

"Fuck!" I groaned. In the middle of me enjoying Butta's sweet nectar, she took my whole dick in her mouth along with a ball.

"Shit!" I moaned into her pussy. Looking at Royce, you wouldn't think she knew how to suck a dick, but shawty was giving super head a run for her money. She figure-eighted my shit, starting at the balls and going to the tip.

"AHHHHH WHAT THE FUCK!" I screamed, pushing Royce off of me. While she was sucking, her teeth sank into the head of my penis. At first, I thought she was just trying to apply pressure until the pain I felt grew worse.

"That's for pointing that damn gun in my face. You think I forgot because you made me cum. Karma, I'm only gonna tell you this shit once; don't you ever in your life think about doing that shit again. You saying I was trying to set you up was enough disrespect. I care for you and even though I may not agree with what you do, I understand why you do it. Next time, learn how to talk to me about things, instead of acting irrationally," she said.

"Man, you had to bite my dick to say all that shit? It could've waited until after I busted my nut or something."

"Oh, you gonna bust your nut because I'm ready to explode. I just had to say that before we went any further. There's no going back after this." She pointed between me and her and I smirked.

"The fuck you saying."

"I'm saying that it's me and you until the end. Ain't no other bitch getting my dick." She giggled. "That's how y'all niggas say it, right?"

"You need to stop reading them damn urban fiction books. The fuck you reading 'bout thugs for when you got one right here?"

"Oh, you a thug, huh? Then, come give me some of that thug lovin." She smiled. I got off the couch and stood in front of her, placing my finger in her dimple.

"That's what you want?"

"Yes."

"Turn around and assume the position against the door ma." I smacked her ass, putting a little pep in her step.

Her back was arched as her hands were stretched out as far as they would go. I walked up behind her, biting the back of her neck. Lifting her ass up, I placed my dick at her entrance.

"Push back," I demanded.

"AHHHHHH SHHHHHHIIIIIITTTTT!" she moaned when I entered her.

I placed my hands perfectly on her hips and went to work. I wasn't pumping fast like these whack ass niggas be doing. I pumped fast enough, so she would be excited every time I hit her spot but slow enough that she felt everything. Her shit was tight as a Chinese finger trap and if you ever got your fingers stuck in one of those, then you understand what I'm saying.

"I'm cumming Karma, bayyyybeyyyyyyyy!"

Butta started throwing her ass back wildly as she met every thrust. The way she was panting and moaning had me going crazy. I promise if I wouldn't have bit down on my bottom lip, a nigga would've moaned like a straight bitch. Butta's juices began to flow and that was the end of the story. I pumped one last time, going as deep as I could, releasing all in her.

"Damn, I don't even have a change of clothes," she sighed, trying to catch her breath.

"You can throw on my sweats and a t-shirt. We going back to the crib anyway."

"Uh, we are supposed to be going out to the club."

"I'm not going to the club and neither are you. So, tell Callie she on her own."

"Ugh, you're no fun," she pouted.

I pulled her into my arms and kissed her on the forehead. "I'm not supposed to be fun. Go in the drawers in the bedroom and find something for you to put on, so we can head out of here. I'ma be upstairs with everyone else."

"Okay, I'll let you know when I'm done."

"Ight ma." I kissed her one last time before letting her go.

When she disappeared into the room, I left out the apartment. As I made my way to the trap, I had to shake my head because this shit was fuckin' crazy. Who would've thought Karma would be falling for a chick; the shit was unreal. I still felt bad about the whole gun situation, so I was going to do something nice for her.

I walked in the apartment and the only person that was left was Trench.

"Is everything ight?" he asked me.

I nodded my head yeah and snatched up the money to take home and count. I usually didn't travel with large sums of money but the whole shit that went down between Trench and I had me feeling uneasy. Trench really had been on one lately and I wasn't feeling that shit. I was going to keep my eye on him, just in case he was up to some foul shit.

Chapter 17: Royce

"So, when am I going to meet the man that got you walking in here glowing?" my mother asked as I walked in the door.

After changing clothes yesterday, I spent the night with Karma. I would've still been with him, but he told me had something to do.

"Ma, I think it's too early in the relationship to be bringing him home," I told her, closing the door and sitting on the couch with her. I sat my bag down and crossed my legs, sitting Indian style.

"It's too soon for me to meet him, but it isn't too soon for you to be fucking him." The way she looked at me caused me to put my head down.

"Don't put your head down because the deed is already done. What you thought, you were going to walk in here and I wasn't going to notice the slight limp in your walk. You are my child, which means I know you better than anyone. Now Royce, I'm not judging. I'm just making sure that you are aware of your actions."

"Ma, I'm fully aware of what I'm doing-" I went to explain, but she cut me off with a raise of her hand.

"No Royce, I don't think you do. You may think you are taking things slow with him, but I see otherwise. This young man got you all caught up and shit. Granted, he is making you happy because you walk around here as if you're floating on cloud nine, but you don't think everything that is happening is too soon?"

"Ma, I don't understand what the problem is. You said it yourself that he is making me happy, why isn't that enough?" I sighed. My mother was blowing mine with everything she was saying. She was acting as if Karma had me under some type of spell and he was making do things that I didn't want to do.

"The problem is that you just got out of a relationship and now you are head over heels in another one. Has your heart even full mended from the six-year relationship with Addison? Or is the sex too good that you don't even remember your heart is broken?"

"Ma!" I yelled.

"Don't Ma me, I'm being serious Royce."

"No, I haven't forgot about my heart being broken; I just don't see a point in dwelling on it. Time heals all wounds so in time, I will be okay. I thought me moving on is what you wanted?"

"You moving on is what I wanted for, you but I didn't want you moving on to where you lose yourself in another man. So many young girls don't take the time after a break up to find themselves and who they are, so when they get into a new relationship, they allow the same things to happen."

"Ma I'm not these normal young girls. I know what I deserve and I'm not accepting anything less. I know you just want the best for me and I love you for that, but everything I got going on with Karma is good. Matter of fact, it's real good."

"Okay, I won't say anything else about it for now. You're happy and that's all that matters. I expect to see him for dinner soon though. You brought Addison over two weeks into y'all dating."

"That was different. I was in high school when Addison and I started dating; I didn't really know anything about men."

"You mean to say boy because Addison is not a man." My mother laughed.

"You are right on that one," I agreed.

"Just make sure that you stay protected when you are doing the do."

"I'm always protected, trust me," I told her.

"Yeah okay. Now, get out so I can finish watching my stories."

I playfully rolled my eyes at my mother, picked up my bag, and headed for my bedroom. Placing my bag of clothes on my hamper, I jumped in my bed tired as hell, and my body was sore. As soon as we stepped foot in Karma's house, we were all over each other. Neither one of us could get enough of the other. The only reason we stopped was because Karma had money to count. Instead of going to sleep, I took a quick shower, then helped him count his money. We were counting into the wee hours of the morning.

When we finished, we took like a two-hour nap, went another round, then we were out the door. In the car ride to my house, we made idle chat that really wasn't about anything. I didn't know if he could tell or not, but I was still uncomfortable about the whole gun situation. Yeah, I played it off like I wasn't mad anymore but, deep down, I was frightened. That was the first time I ever had a gun pointed at me. I never thought I would be in that situation, let alone my boyfriend be the dude holding the gun. I was going to ask Karma what made him think I was a snitch but felt as though I might have been overstepping my boundaries. Sooner or later, we were going to have a conversation about this because boyfriend or no boyfriend, I wasn't going to tolerate looking death in the face again.

∞ ∞ ∞

"Royce, Callie is at the door and I'm leaving out for work," my mother said, walking into my bedroom.

"Alright, tell her I will be right out. Have a good day at work," I told her. After waking up from my nap, I decided to jump in the shower. I planned on playing the crib because I didn't have any other plans. Karma hadn't text me or call me to let me know he finished handling his business and neither did Callie, which was why I didn't understand why she decided to just pop up.

"Love you." My mother blew me a kiss, then left out.

"I really need to find a side job until I go back to school," I said out loud to myself.

My mother made good money at her job, so I didn't have to pay bills or anything. All she wanted from me was to get that college degree. My money would go to things like clothes, food, and if I wanted to go out. The money I saved from my tutoring job was still there, but I didn't want to touch it anymore. I wanted to save that up to either get a car or move out after I graduated. I was definitely going to start looking for something because in a sense, my mother was right. I needed to find myself and some time away from Karma might be good. I would miss him, but I still needed time for me too.

I finished dressing, then went into the living room. Callie was stretched out on the couch like she lived here.

"You mind putting your feet down lil mama," I told her, sitting on the love seat.

"Took you long enough to get dressed."

"I mean when someone doesn't call or text to let the other person know they coming over, how are they supposed to know they have to rush."

"I didn't call because I didn't plan on coming over here, but then I figured my news was just too big to not tell you in person."

"Okay, so what's the news?" I smiled. Callie seemed happy, so I was going to be happy for her. I wondered where she went last night because when I met up with Karma, it was only him and Trench in the apartment.

"Smitty took me out to dinner," she beamed.

"Really!" I squealed. "How did that happen?"

"Well, after you and Karma left, Trench and I started going back and forth because I had a feeling it was his bitch ass who told Karma you were a rat. Things got heated and Smitty pulled me away, taking me outside. One thing led to another and we ended up having dinner together. Royce, when I tell you it was everything, please believe me that it was everything. Our conversation just flowed so well and everything was perfect," she sighed.

"That's good. Where did y'all go?"

"To Applebee's. I know it's not nothing fancy, but I don't expect anything fancy when he has a chick at home. We are just in the get to know each other-"

"Wait, he has a chick at home? How do you even know that?"

"I ran into them at the gas station but that's not important. What's important is that we had a wonderful date."

"Um, I hope you are going to leave his ass alone," I told her. I knew how it felt to get cheated on. I didn't know Smitty's girl, but I would hate for her to go through the same heart break I went through.

"Why would I do that when I just found out that he is interested in me?"

"Come on Callie, don't do that?"

"Don't do what?"

"Don't be that chick who steals the dude just because you want him and he's giving you attention. I know how it feels to get cheated on and I wouldn't want that for his chick."

"Oh, so you care more about his bitch's feelings then mine?"

"No, I don't mean that. I'm just saying how would you feel if someone tried to steal a dude from you."

"I wouldn't feel no type of way because no bitch would be better at doing the shit I do for my nigga. I would have that nigga eating my ass before he thinks about fucking with another bitch."

"Okay Callie. It's good to see that you're confident," I said, giving up. At the end of the day, Callie was going to do what she wanted to do anyway.

"Confident is the only way to be, especially with the men that we are dealing with. Karma is next in line and everyone knows it. Mo' money, mo' problems, remember that."

"I'm not worried about it," I told her.

"Okay." She laughed.

"Are you going to the Cracked Mug tonight?" Callie asked. I was surprised because she doesn't usually ask about the coffee house. She claimed it would cramp her style.

"Yeah, but I need to do something with this hair of mine. Karma had his hands all in my shit and now it looks wild as hell." I fingered combed what was left of my twist-out from the day before.

"Why was Karma's hands in your hair?" Her words trailed off, then she jumped while looking at me. I guess she put two and two together and figured it out.

"OH MY GOD! You let him hit!" she screamed.

"Shut up before you tell the whole building," I told her.

"Oh my gosh girl, I'm so happy for you. That's why you glowing and shit."

"It's not even all that serious." I tried to play it off, but I was just as happy as she was.

"It is that fucking serious. Man, tell me how it was."

"Uh, no."

"Why not? You told me about Addison."

"That's because the sex was mediocre."

"Mhmm, that must mean Karma's fine ass put it down."

"Draw your own conclusion," I said shyly.

"Well, let me put some bantu knots in your hair. Then, when we get to the coffee house, you can take them out."

"Okay." I walked into my room and grabbed all the hair stuff I needed.

Going back in the living, I saw Callie texting on her phone with a smile on her face. I didn't approve of what she was doing, but I already spoke my peace.

"You singing tonight?" Callie asked, putting her phone down.

"I don't know. Maybe, but who knows."

"I think you should sing."

"Since when do you care about me singing at The Cracked Mug?"

"I don't care about you singing at The Cracked Mug but you have a beautiful voice. Shit, when Smitty and I get married, you can be our wedding singer along with my maid of honor."

"You are crazy as hell, you know that." I laughed.

"You call it crazy; I call it speaking it into existence. On the real, I think you should sing something cute."

"I don't know but I'll think about it."

Callie didn't say anything else about the whole singing thing as she finished up my hair. I didn't plan on singing, but I guess I might as well get up there and sing something. Singing was just something I did for fun because I loved it. I never thought about making it a career because then it would feel more like a job.

It took Callie an hour to finish my hair and then after that, we got dressed and headed out. On the way to The Cracked Mug, I sent Karma a quick text, letting him know where I was going to be. I intentionally was going to tell him that I missed him, but my mother's voice kept ringing in my head about me getting wrapped up in him. My mother was right about me being caught up in Karma because he definitely had me in my feelings.

Chapter 18: Karma

I had never been so fuckin' nervous in my life until at this moment. I dropped Butta off, then went and handled the little business I had. Once everything was squared away, I went to go see Red. I ran everything down to him about the Trench situation and me pulling out on Butta. Man, Red let my ass have it. He went in on me because I was dead wrong. I respected Red because he was like my father, so I took everything he handed to me. When it was all said and done, he told me I needed to do something big for Butta to make it up to her.

I already knew I needed to do something but didn't know what. I ran a couple of ideas by Red but none of them seemed good enough. I ended up telling him about how she liked to sing at The Cracked Mug. Leave it to Red to know the owner of the place. Red worked his magic and now Royce was the entertainment every Thursday night. I thought that shit was perfect because she loved to sing and why not get paid for something that you love to do.

I wanted to surprise Royce with the news, so I hit up Callie and told her to make sure Royce would be there tonight. Before Callie agreed, she went off on my ass for that gun shit. I half listened to her bitchin' and was happy as hell when she agreed to the plan. Fast forward hours later, here I was backstage about to get on stage and embarrass myself, all for Royce.

"I can't believe you about to do this shit. I have to meet this girl 'cause she has to be something special." Red laughed.

"Shut the fuck up." I laughed. "The way I'm feeling, I might not even make it on stage." As soon as those words came out my mouth, Callie texted me, letting me know they were here and sitting up front.

"Man, she here," I told Red.

"Then nigga, get it together because I'm about to go and announce you."

Red left and went on stage. I grabbed a bottle of water and chugged that shit.

"This young man that's comin' to the stage is about to do something he's never done before, so don't go too hard on him. Welcome to the stage, my son, Karma."

I coolly walked on stage, even though I was shitting bricks. There had to be at least a hundred people in the place tonight and the only person I saw was Butta. She looked surprised as hell to see me up here. I winked at her then grabbed the mic, ready to get this shit over with. The music came on. Beyoncé's soft voice came through the speakers as I ran my hands over my face.

"I can't believe I'm doing this shit," I thought, just as the beat dropped in; my que.

"I'm an outlaw, got an outlaw chick. Bumping 2pac, on my outlaw shit. Matching tatts, this ink don't come off. Even if rings come off, if things ring off. My nails get dirty, my past ain't purtty, my lady is, my Mercedes is."

My rapping wasn't A1 but shit, I was better than some of those things that were out today. I swagged out to the music as I continued to rap. The whole time I was going in, I made sure that my eyes stayed on Royce.

"Touch a nigga where his rib at, I click clat. Push your motherfucking wig back, I did that. I been wildin' since a juvi, she was a good girl 'til she knew me. Now she in the drop bussin' u'e. Screaming…" I reached out, pulling Royce on stage and passed her the mic.

She beautifully sang the hook as I stared into her beautiful eyes. This shit was so unreal but that's how every day felt fucking with Royce. Y'all niggas can call me soft or whatever, but I was speaking true shit. Red came out and passed me another mic quickly, right before it was time for me to bring it home.

"Deeper than words, beyond right. Die for your love, beyond life. Sweet as a Jesus piece, beyond ice. Blind me baby with your neon lights. Ray Bans on, police in sight. Oh, what a beautiful death, let's both wear white. If you go to heaven and they bring me to hell, just sneak out and meet me, bring a box of L's. They ain't see potential in me girl, but you see it. If it's me and you against the world, then so be it."

Royce finished off the song and when everything was done, the crowd cheered, giving us a standing ovation. I wrapped my arms around Butta, pulling her close to me.

"That shit was embarrassing as hell but, for you, I would do anything."

"I love you, Karma. I know it's too soon to say but it's how I feel. You got me all caught up in my feelings and until just now, I didn't know that what I was feeling was love."

"I love you too, Butta"

I kissed her deeply and the crowd went crazy. She melted into my embrace, giggling into my chest. I pulled her off the stage and into the back.

"I can't believe you did that shit. Man, you growing up my nigga," Red said as soon as he saw us.

"Butta, I want you to meet someone. Butta, this is Red and Red, this is Royce."

"I been waiting to meet the young lady that turned my young bull into a soft ass lamb." Red laughed.

"It's nice to meet you." Butta blushed. Red pulled her into a hug.

"Chill out old head; you hugging her a little too tight for comfort," I told him.

"Shut that shit up." Red laughed. "Did Mr. Jealous over there tell you that you would be the entertainment every Thursday night?"

"Wait, what?" Butta asked, looking from Red to me.

"You could've gave me a chance to at least tell her. I know how much you love singing and I wanted to surprise you with something special. Red helped set everything up tho, so I guess it's as much of his surprise as it is mine."

"I don't even know what to say."

"Just say all that money you gonna be making you will save up and use it to do something big when you graduate," I told her.

"That's a given." She smiled, leaping into my arms.

While Royce and I hugged, Red stood back looking like a proud parent. I owed a lot to Red because if it wasn't for him, I would probably be six feet under. Since I've known Red, he had never asked me for anything until we had that talk. All he wanted was for me to not let the game consume me and to find happiness outside of it. I was going to take heed to his words and honor that wish.

Chapter 19: Royce

I was too excited when Karma told me that I would be the entertainment on Thursday nights. Not to mention, I was going to get paid for it, which was a plus. I thought Karma telling me he loved me was going to be the icing on the cake, but this news took it all. I was beyond geeked. I went as far as thanking both Red and Karma multiple times.

"Girl, guess what?" I said to Callie once I made it back to her table. Red wanted Karma to walk him out, so I went to share my news with Callie.

"You don't have to tell me because I already know. I helped set everything up." She cheesed.

"You didn't?" I said shocked.

"Yes I did. When have you known me to ever care about The Cracked Mug." She giggled, getting up and hugging me. "I'm so happy for you, best friend."

"I can't believe you kept it from me. This kind of makes me wonder what else you are keeping from me," I fake pouted, sitting down.

"You don't even believe that shit coming out your mouth. You know everything there is to know."

I looked at her, playfully rolling my eyes. "If you say so."

"I do so that's the final word." She laughed. I joined in on the laughter but it didn't last for long.

"Royce!" The sound of his voice caused me to cringe because I knew this happiness I was feeling was about to be gone.

"Is that Addison?" Callie asked.

"Yeah, that's his ass. Come on and let's go outside where Karma's at. I don't want no issues."

Callie agreed and we got up in left. Us leaving didn't stop Addison because he followed us outside, still calling my name. Karma was in my view but something told me to get rid of Addison before Karma seen him.

"Addison, what do you want?" I asked him, turning around. Callie stood off to the side but close enough, just in case I needed her.

"I'm just trying to talk to you. You too good to have a conversation with me or something"

"It's not even like that Addison; I just don't see anything for us to talk about. You moved on and so have I. Tell ole girl I'm sorry about her nose; that was a different me."

"Who the fuck you moved on with Royce!"

"Addison, stop yelling," I panicked.

"DON'T TELL ME TO STOP YELLING. I NEED TO KNOW WHO THE FUCK IS SLIPPING THEIR DICK IN MY PUSSY AT NIGHT!" he continued yelling and drawing attention to us.

I didn't even want to look behind me where Karma was because I was damn near positive that he was coming over this way.

"Girl, Karma is comin' over here and he don't look the least bit pleased," Callie confirmed what I already knew.

Karma walked right up to me, draping his arm over my shoulder. I couldn't even bring my eyes to meet his as I felt his gaze on me for a second.

"I'm the nigga that's been up in yo pussy; do we got a problem?" Karma asked.

"The fuck you mean do we got a problem? Hell yeah, we got a problem. Who the fuck is you?" Addison was talking that talk, but I knew for a fact that he couldn't back it up. If things escalated, I would bet my bottom dollar that Addison's ass would be laid out on the ground.

"Addison, please just leave me alone. We are no longer together and my sex life is no longer your concern."

"I was the first dude to get all up in that. What you have in between your legs will always be my concern."

"You may be the first but, nigga, I'm the last."

Karma politely moved me out the way, then sent two punches to Addison's face, causing him to fall to the ground. Callie rushed to my side as Karma yanked Addison off the ground by the collar of his shirt.

"Nigga, I told yo ass before, I don't do this talkin' shit. I bust my nines-"

"Karma. No!" I screamed out, cutting him off. "He's not even worth it baby, just let him be," I pleaded. There was no way I was going to let Karma commit a murder with over a hundred witnesses watching him.

"Nigga, you lucky," Karma said, throwing him to the ground. "But you ain't that lucky."

With nothing but ease, he swiftly pulled out his gun and shot Addison in between his legs. I went to let out a scream, but Callie quickly covered my mouth.

"ARGHHHHH!" Addison cried out in agonizing pain.

"Shut yo bitch ass up; you lucky I only shot you in your dick and not your heart." Karma turned towards me and all the anger that he had in his face subsided.

"Royce and Callie, let's go," he said.

Sirens could be heard in the distance, so he didn't have to tell us twice. We rushed over to the car and jumped in. Karma speed off without saying anything. I was still in a state of shock while Callie texted me about how amazed she was.

"What you over there thinkin' 'bout?" Karma asked, looking at me through the corner of his eye.

"Did you really have to shot him in the dick?"

"That honestly shouldn't be any of your concern; you don't plan on fuckin' or suckin' his bitch ass, right?"

"Of course not."

"Ight, then be happy I shot him in the dick instead of killin' him."

For me, there wasn't even a point in continue with the conversation. Addison brought this on himself; I just hoped this time around he would stay away because I doubt I would be able to save him twice.

"Callie, you can stay here tonight, and we all can go out for breakfast in the morning," Karma said, getting out his car.

We went into the house and Karma showed Callie to her room. After making sure Callie was straight, we headed for his bedroom.

"Let me ask you something?"

"Go ahead," I told him.

"You fuckin' with me right?" he asked, raising his eyebrow.

"Yeah, what made you ask that?"

"You the first female I ever said those three words to. I need to make sure that what we got is real because I'm doing shit out the ordinary and I don't need to be doing it for nothing. Any other dude would've been left breathless but off the strength of you, I let him make it. I'm all about you; I just need to know you all about a nigga too. If you still got feelings for your ex, that's cool and I'll step, but that's some shit you have to let me know now 'cause if I find out some shit, I'm sending one to his head and two to yours for being disloyal."

I didn't even know what to say because he basically just told me he would kill me. Did I plan on messing with Addison? Hell no, so Karma didn't have anything to worry about.

"I'm not even lookin' for a response, so your silence is-"

"You may not be lookin' for a response, but I have one. You may not want to say it but I understand you are worried about getting hurt. I understand that your mother didn't love you, so you try to make it seem like everyone is like her. Well, guess what? I'm not. I love you and I plan on loving you until I'm old and gray. Yeah, we only been dating for a month and a half, but all I see is you. My love for you is real so don't ever question it."

"I hear you talkin' Butta," he smirked.

"Yeah, you hear me talkin' but are you understanding what I'm saying?"

"I understand you, Royce. Look at you trying to take charge." He laughed, mushing me.

"I only take charge when I feel the need to."

"Come get in the shower with me, so I can bend that ass over."

"I guess I can make that happen." I laughed and headed for the bathroom.

The deeper Karma and I got pulled into this relationship, the deeper my feelings became. We were both taking chances on each other, but Karma didn't have anything to worry about because me hurting him would never happen.

Chapter 20: Callie

My ass couldn't sleep with all the noise Karma and Royce was making; if her hot ass kept it up, she was going to turn up pregnant. I turned the tv on and made sure to turn it all the way up to drown out their sex session. I couldn't front; the sex noise they were making had me hornier than ever.

"I shouldn't have cut Trench off," I said out loud to myself.

If Trench was good for one thing, it was definitely scratching this cat. I guess I was going to have to handle things on my own. I grabbed my phone and was about to head to the bathroom when an even better idea came to mind. Dialing Smitty's number, I laid back down on the bed and got comfortable.

"Wassup."

"Uh, it's Callie," I said.

"Wassup ma? I didn't expect you to be using my number so soon."

"I figured what's a better time than the present." When we were leaving Applebee's, we exchanged numbers and promised to get up later in the week. Shit, twenty-four hours was good enough for me.

"Wassup, what you calling for?" What he said didn't come off as rude, but it didn't come off as friendly either.

"Nothing, I just wanted to see if you wanted to chill or something."

"It's late as hell and you calling me to chill. Tell me what you really want Callie?"

"I want you," I said and held my breath, waiting for his response. No dude has ever had me scared to say what I want, but Smitty had me nervous as hell.

"That's your word?"

"Yeah."

"Word around town is that you get down a lot for the right price and just cause I got it, don't mean I'm trickin.'"

"You can't believe everything you hear in the street."

"You right about that, but you also can't trust a woman that has a motive."

"Okay, I see this going nowhere, so I'm just going to say have a nice night."

"Hol' up," he said, stopping me from hanging up.

"If you gonna keep insulting me, then you might as well let me hang up because I don't want to hear it. Not to mention, I'm sure your girlfriend isn't gonna like the fact you getting late night calls." I threw his girlfriend in the mix because I was feeling hella salty. How this nigga gonna try to throw in my face what the streets said about me when we were just vibin' twenty-four hours ago?

"You weren't worried about my girl when you called so don't worry about her ass now. Where you at?"

"I'm at Karma's crib, why?" I sassed.

"Callie, kill that attitude and shit because you not even mad right now. You probably smiling hard as fuck at the fact that we about to meet up and you gonna get this dick. That's what you want right, this dick?"

"Wha... what?" I stuttered.

"You heard me, you got your car or nah?"

"No," I sighed. I was kicking myself in the ass for not driving my own car over here.

"Damn Callie, you fuckin' up but I'll tell you what. I'ma come over and pick you up to take you out to breakfast, then we can go do what it do before I have to get back to the money."

"I don't know if I can wait that long," I pouted. My pussy was throbbing and it only wanted one thing from one person.

"You honestly don't have a choice. Call me in the morning when you ready to go," he demanded and hung up.

I saw there with my panties soaking wet from that shit he just did. If it's one thing I loved, it was when a man took control. Yeah, Smitty was spoken for, but that was only for the time being. I had every intention on rocking his world tomorrow morning. When I got done with him, he wasn't gonna know what to do with himself. I was about to tat my name all up, down, and around that dick. I was gonna claim what's mine.

∞ ∞ ∞

Waking up the next morning, the first thing I did was go knocking on Karma and Royce's door. I needed to wash my ass, but I needed some feminine products. The first couple of times no one answered, so I banged louder. I wasn't trying to wake anyone up but, at the same time, I was.

"Callie, why are you banging on the door like you don't have no sense? It's only eight in the morning. When do you ever get up this early?" Royce asked. She stepped outside of the room and closed the door behind her.

"When I'm trying to get some dick. I need to get in the shower and I don't know where anything is."

"Go in the linen closet to the left and grab the towel and wash clothes. The cabinet next to it has the Dove soap in it."

"Okay, but where do you keep the Summer Eve's products?"

"What do you mean Summer Eve's? I don't keep that stuff over here; the hell you need that for anyway?" She yawned.

"Don't even worry about it," I told her.

I rushed to the cabinets that she told me to look in and grabbed everything I needed. I wanted to douche just to feel extra fresh down there, but this Dove soap would have to do. Plus, people said all you really need is water to clean your vagina anyway. Getting in the shower, I took my time, making sure to wash every nook and cranny. I was gonna be wearing last night's outfit, but at least I was going to be clean.

161

I got out and headed back to the cabinet to find some lotion. The only thing that was in there was some type of coconut oil lotion. It wasn't what I was looking for, but it was gonna have to do. I ran back to my room, lotioned up, and got redressed. My vixen sew-in was in need of touch up. There wasn't much I could do at the moment besides brushing it out and throwing it into a ponytail. I looked at myself in the mirror, not really liking what I saw but hey, it was good enough. Smitty knew what I looked like on a good day, so I wasn't worried. Pussy didn't have a face; I was sure he wasn't gonna be choosey because of my appearance.

"Callie, are you dressed?" Royce asked from the other side of the door.

"Yeah," I sang out.

"Karma is gonna take us out to breakfast, then he will take you to your car. Smitty is supposed to be meeting us there too." Just the mention of Smitty's name had me hot and bothered.

"Okay, that's fine." I smiled.

"We just have to shower and get dressed, then we can go. You have bags under your eyes; did you get any sleep?"

"How could anyone sleep with all your loud moans and screams?" I smirked.

"Oh my gosh, you heard that?" she asked, bringing her hand to her mouth.

"Yeah, I heard you. Karma had to be putting that dick on you."

"I plead the fifth." She laughed.

"I bet your ass do. Anyway, hurry up so we can go eat and stuff."

"What are you in such a rush for and whose dick are you supposed to be getting?"

"I'm going to keep that little bit of information to myself until I'm sure about things. I just want to see this situation out without any judgement or anything."

"Well, I'm not one to judge because look at how fast things have been moving with Karma and I. I still haven't introduced him to my mom."

"Why haven't you introduced him to your mom yet?"

"I don't know; she keeps bringing up the fact that we are moving too fast and just like you, I don't want to be judged. I didn't set out looking for a relationship, it kind of just happened. I'm honestly happy it happened because I can only imagine how I would be if I didn't have someone showing me how a woman should be treated."

"Well, at some point, you have to introduce him because besides me, your mother is the most important person in your life."

"I know, I know. I'll take him over there later today if he's free," she sighed.

"Make sure you let me know how that goes. Now, go get dressed," I told her, pushing her out my room.

She stuck up the middle finger at me while giggling and walking away. As soon as she was gone, I closed the door and rushed over to my phone. Scrolling to Smitty's name, I sent him a text, letting him know I looked forwarded to seeing him. I waited, checking my phone every five minutes, but never got a response. I was hurt but, at the same time, I said fuck it because I was about to see him at breakfast.

Chapter 21: Karma

"Nigga, where you at?" I asked Smitty. Royce, Callie, and I were standing in the Ihop parking lot, waiting on this nigga to come.

"I'm pulling up now, chill out." He laughed.

I hung up the phone and pulled Royce closer to me. Butta was honestly my safe haven; I couldn't see life without her in it.

"I want you to meet my mother," she said, staring at me.

"Ight, just let me know when."

"How is tonight?" she asked.

"I can't tonight; I have to hold shit down." As soon as the words I can't left my mouth, she started pouting and making this ugly ass face.

"Fix yo face Butta. You ugly as hell when you make that face," I joked.

"And you're just ugly period." She laughed.

"You don't even believe that."

"Whatever, just let me know when you are free because my mother has been asking about you lately."

"Oh, your moms really wants to meet the kid huh?"

"I guess so." She playfully rolled her eyes, then pushed me away and went to stand next to Callie.

Five minutes later, Smitty finally showed his face and we all headed inside. The hostess showed us to our seat and handed us the menus. For the most part, breakfast was chill; we ate and made idle chit chat. Smitty and Callie were on a whole different level. I didn't know exactly what was going on with the two of them, but the vibe they had between each other was strong as fuck. I hoped like hell they weren't fucking because that shit would be crazy. Trench didn't want to admit it but he was feeling Callie, so for Smitty to be knocking her down would be some shit.

"I'ma take Callie to her car," Smitty said once we made it back to the parking lot.

"Ight, that's cool with-"

"Hey Karma," the soft voice said. Without turning in the direction of the person, I already knew who it was.

"Wassup Camellia, what you doing here?" I asked her.

"Nothing, following my no good boyfriend here. Come to find out the nigga been cheating on me with some dusty bitch."

"You need us to handle him?" I offered. She was family, so it was only right that I held her down because she held me down on more than one occasion.

"Nah, it's cool; his bitch doesn't hold a candle to this flame. But who is this pretty gem?" she asked, staring at Butta. Before I could even attempt to introduce the two, Royce butted in.

"The name is Royce and you are?"

"No one you need to concern yourself with," Camellia smirked.

"Camellia, you need to chill the fuck out with that smart shit; it's not even needed."

"Oops, look at you putting me in my place." She laughed. "If I offended you, Beamer, my bad, and it's nice to meet you Toyota." She smiled, then walked off.

"Did that bitch just call me Toyota?" Callie asked.

"Pay her ass no mind Callie. Karma, you need to get rid of that broad; there are a million and one bitches in the hood that can do what she do," Smitty said.

"Karma, I'm ready to go." I turned and looked at Royce, trying to figure out who she was talking to in that tone of voice.

"Watch your tone of voice Butta. That shit wasn't even that deep. You already know Camellia plays all day every day."

"I don't care if she plays all day, that shit was rude as fuck and if I run into that hoe again, I'm going to beat that ass," Callie huffed.

"Let's get the fuck out of here," I said.

"Callie, this the hoe shit that you doing? You dropped me for that fuckin' nigga. Damn Smitty, I didn't know we had static and shit!" Trench yelled, coming out of nowhere. The fuck was today; pop up on Karma and the crew day or some shit?

Trench walked up on Smitty, knocking Callie to the ground. "Trench, are you out of your fucking mind!" Callie screamed, getting up.

"Shut the fuck up hoe, real nigga talking. Smitty, if you wanted a taste of the bitch, all you had to do was speak. I would've passed her loose pussy ass right over."

"Nigga, the fuck is you talking about? Because I'm out with a bitch, I have to be fucking her or some shit. I already have a situation going on, so a nigga isn't pressed for pussy but obviously, yo ass is."

"Nobody over here is pressed for pussy because a nigga is making real boss moves and shit. That money always has and always will be the motive."

"Then, what you out here showing yo ass for?" Smitty laughed.

"I'm trying to figure out if you like the taste of my dick." Trench laughed and Smitty hit that nigga clean in his mouth. Trench stumbled some, spit out some blood from his mouth, then squared up. The two were going pound for pound and blow for blow. Somehow, Callie's little ass jumped on Trench's back, sending blows of her own. I quickly grabbed Callie and slung her ass over to where Royce was standing.

"Royce, go get in the car and take your fucking friend with you." I threw her the keys and turned my back towards her.

I stood there for a little, letting these two niggas blow of this steam and animosity they have towards each other. Royce ended up zooming past us, leaving the parking lot.

"Ight, that's enough!" I yelled, getting in between the two.

"Nah Karma, move the fuck out the way. His ugly ass wants to test a nigga over some bitch I could give two shits about. This nigga deserve this ass whoopin'; maybe it will teach him how to be a man about his shit."

"Nigga, fuck you!" Trench spat, wiping blood from his mouth. "Karma, you supposed to be my nigga and you right with this nigga doing wrong and shit."

"Nigga, what you talking about? You out here acting like a fool because we all went to breakfast together? Get the fuck out yo feelings. If you knew how to keep them muthafuckers in check, you would've been invited too."

"Ain't nobody in they fuckin' feelings but you niggas. It's cool though because a nigga is 'bout to come up."

"Nigga, you ain't about to do shit but continue licking the shit off Karma's shoes. Everyone know you ain't shit without him, so pipe all that shit down." Smitty laughed.

Trench tried to charge Smitty, but I pushed him back. This shit was getting out of hand and I wasn't here for it.

"Chill the fuck out nigga, damn. Y'all out here fighting like bitches and for what?"

"Straight up, fuck you and that nigga Karma. I don't need either one of y'all ass. I'm gonna eat regardless. Fuck out of here. Watch what I tell you; I'm making big moves and when shit comes down and I'm the nigga in charge, don't try and jump on my bandwagon either." Trench looked at us one last time before storming off.

"Man, don't even trip off that nigga" Smitty laughed.

"Just shut the fuck up and bring me to the spot," I told him.

His laughter ended real quick as we jumped in his car and he pulled off. Turning my phone off because I didn't want to be bothered, I closed my eyes while trying to process everything that happened.

I knew I was gonna have to deal with Royce because of that shit Camellia did. Man, Camellia was a funny ass character but she was cool as hell, which was why I didn't feed into the bullshit she did when she called Royce Beamer. All she wanted was to get a rise out of Royce to see how far she would be able to go with her. Camellia was the shit at what she did and I wasn't trying to fuck with anyone new. I was gonna have a talk with her and make sure she knew not to overstep her boundaries with that funny shit. I was never going to put another bitch over Royce but, at the same time, they both were gonna have to cut that catty shit out.

Smitty and Trench were gonna have to stop with the catty shit too. Trench was over here acting like a straight bitch over a female he didn't want to admit he had real feelings for. I didn't know what was going on between Smitty and Callie, so it wasn't my place to speak on it. The way I saw it this was something Smitty and Trench was gonna have to work through. I figured I would give Trench a couple of days to cool down. All that shit he said about making moves and shit wasn't even fazing me because that nigga wasn't going nowhere. Shit, I hoped he wasn't going nowhere because disloyalty ended in bloodshed in my eyes.

Chapter 22: Royce

"That Camellia bitch seems so familiar, but I can't put my finger on where I know her from," Callie complained.

"I'm so tired of hearing that bitch's name," I spat.

"Oh, did her calling you Beamer get you that mad?" Callie laughed. I grilled Callie, then turned my attention back to the road.

"Don't look at me like that; all I'm saying is if you had a problem with what she said, then maybe you should've said something."

"It wasn't my place to say anything. If I would've said something, it wouldn't have made a difference. Bitches like her only respect when a dude sticks up for his girl, especially when the dude used to fuck the bitch who was in the wrong. I'm not dumb, that bitch was testing to see how far she could get saying slick shit."

"I don't need no man sticking up for me because I will pop a bitch in her mouth."

"Don't try to play like I'm scared to throw my hands, but I know if I would've hit her, we would've been fighting every time we seen each other. I'm telling you, a woman who used to fuck your man only chill when the man puts them in their place because the woman don't see you as shit but some new pussy he getting."

"That kinda makes sense."

"It makes a whole lot of sense," I told her.

I wasn't all the way pissed off, but I was annoyed. I didn't care for Camellia at all; she was disrespectful as hell and had this arrogance about her. The whole spying on her boyfriend thing she said was straight bullshit if you asked me. Karma seemed surprised that she even had a boyfriend, that right there told me she was lying. She was up to something foul and I was going to let Karma know.

I pulled up to The Cracked Mug, so Callie could get her car. She jumped out and promised she would call me later. I told her that was cool and drove off, headed to my mother's house. I was hoping like hell she would be sleep when I got in the house. My mother could read me like a book and if she knew I was upset, she was gonna want to have a full conversation about what was wrong. This was an issue I didn't want to bring up to my mother because I didn't want her to have any negative thoughts about Karma before she met him.

I sat out in front of my house for a little while, collectively pulling my thought together. Once I felt I was okay, I got out and walked in the house. I wasn't even two feet in the door before my mother started going in.

"Royce, I know I taught you better than to hang out with dudes who go around killing people."

"Ma, what are you talking about?" I was confused as hell because as far as I knew, Karma hadn't killed anyone, but I wouldn't have put it past him.

"Don't try to play me Royce. Addison's mother called me yesterday and told me how your little boyfriend shot Addison in the genitals."

"Wait, his mom called you? Why would she do that?"

"Apparently, her and her son are worried about the new company you are keeping. Royce, what has happened to you?"

"Ma, nothing has happened to me. I can't say that I'm the same girl I used to be because I have grown since Addison and I broke up. I have Karma to thank for that."

"Oh, so you have grown up in so much in the two or three months that you have been dating Karma." The way his name rolled off her tongue infuriated me. She said it as if his name wasn't even worthy enough to be coming out of her mouth.

"Yes, I have grown up in the last TWO months that we have been dating." My mother had never acted like this before. I felt like I had to defend my relationship to her.

"I don't want you seeing him anymore!" she yelled.

"I am twenty-one years old. You can't tell me who I can and cannot date."

"Like hell I can't. I will not allow my daughter to be with someone who goes around shooting people simply because they are your ex."

"Who told you Karma shot Addison because he was my ex? Karma shot Addison because he was embarrassing me in public. He was talking about my pussy, along with other things. Karma did nothing but defend me and my honor."

"He could've went about it another way. That man didn't have to shoot Addison in his privates. You are lucky they aren't pressing charges against him."

"Addison isn't stupid enough to press charges," I mumbled.

"Yeah because he is scared for his life. I don't want you around that man and that's the end of it. You live in my house; therefore, you obey my rules."

"I don't have to live in your house." I didn't even realize what I was saying until after the words had already came out.

"Then, you can get the hell out Royce. I love you dearly and I want nothing but the best for you."

"How could you want the best for me when you are kicking me out?" I was trying to keep it all together but the tears ended up escaping.

"I need you to see in Karma what I already see. He is not the one for you. The life that he lives isn't you. Do I appreciate him defending your honor, yes, but him shooting Addison was a little too much. What if the bullet would've ricochet and hit you? Would you still be trying to defend him?"

"Ma, that isn't the point."

"Of course that isn't the point. I love you, Royce, but it's now time for me to let you fly. You have learned so much from your relationship with Addison that I just hope you don't make the same mistake twice. Please, just remember the difference between a man who flatters you and a man who compliments you. A man who spends money on you and a man who invests in you. A man who views you as property and a man who views you properly. A man who lusts after you and a man who loves you. Royce, find a man who compliments you, who views you properly, and a man who loves you." My mother gave me a soft kiss on the cheek before walking away from me.

I wanted to call out to her and tell her that it doesn't have to be like this, but my pride wouldn't allow me to. The love I had for Karma wouldn't allow me to stop her. I felt like she was throwing me out in the cold to fend for myself. I didn't want to leave my mother's house, but I didn't see what else I could possibly do. She basically gave me no choice. I didn't want it to seem like I was choosing one over the other because that's not what I was doing. For so long, I had fought for a relationship that was one sided and damaging to my character. This time, though, I was fighting for something more. I was fighting for the love that I felt was real. I was fighting for something true.

I rushed to my room, filling backpacks, duffle bags, and anything else I could find with my stuff. Hours later, when I finished, I sat on my bad and pulled out my phone to call Callie. I didn't want to call Karma because I knew he was out handling business.

"Ahhh hellooo," Callie sang into the phone.

"Callie, I know you didn't answer the phone while you're sexing?' I asked, feeling disgusted.

"I wasn't going to at first but the dude insisted. He said something about it turning him onnnnnnnnnnnnn."

"Ugh bye." I hung up the phone because I wasn't trying to hear that shit. Whoever she was sexing was a straight up freak. Who the hell answers the phone while they are having sex? I took a deep breath as I called the only person I could call at this moment.

"Yo, wassup Butta."

"I need the keys to your house," I sighed.

"What's wrong Royce, you straight?" he asked. I smiled because he had picked up on my mood that quickly.

"Yeah, I'm fine. I just need the keys to your place."

"Ight, come pick them up. I'm over at the spot. When you get here, we gonna talk 'bout whatever is bothering you."

"Okay." I hung up the phone, then started bringing all of my stuff out to the car.

Moving my stuff felt so surreal; I would've never thought my mother and I would be going through something like this. She wasn't even this hard on me when Addison was cheating on me and I still stayed. Once everything was in the car, I went back into the house with the intentions on kissing my mother goodbye. I got to her bedroom door and couldn't do it. I turned around, went into the kitchen, and scribbled a note, letting her know where I was going and that I loved her regardless of everything. A couple of tears slipped down my face as I walked out and got in the car.

I drove off, thinking how I was taking a chance on love and how I hoped it wouldn't fail me.

Chapter 23: Karma

"When she get here, I don't want to hear shit coming out your mouth unless it's an apology," I told Camellia. When I first got here, I called Camellia and told her to come through, so we could talk about that shit that happened earlier.

"Karma, you don't tell me what to do. I'm a grown ass woman that does what she pleases. If your little girlfriend feels some type of way about me getting her name wrong, then that should show you how immature she is because it was an honest mistake."

"Camellia, you and I both know that shit wasn't an honest mistake. Don't forget I know you better than anyone."

"Just as I know you better than anyone, including that chick you think you're in love with."

"That shit is none of your business. You heard what the fuck I said. Keep your mouth closed unless you're apologizing."

"Whatever." She rolled her eyes, but a smirk was plastered on her face.

A text came through on my phone from Royce letting me know she was outside. I got up without saying anything to Camellia and went downstairs to get her. When I got outside, she was still in her car looking a bit dazed. I walked right up and tapped on her window, telling her to unlock the door. I jumped in and just stared at her for a second. Royce's beauty was unremarkable. Everything about her was so simple, yet so complex.

I never saw myself being with a chick like Royce. In a short time, she showed me that love was something worth having and in return, I was going to show her that my love was something worth having.

"Wassup with you, Butta."

"Addison's mom called my mother and told her you shot her son."

"That nigga is such a pussy." I laughed.

"It's not funny Karma. My mother and I got into it because she wanted me to leave you alone. I told her I wouldn't and she kicked me out."

"I'm sorry Butta. I didn't mean to cause any rifts between you and your moms. If you want, I'll go over there right now and fix things."

"No, I'm sure you going over there won't do anything but make things worse."

"Don't even trip because you know I got you, Royce. Things might seem up in the air right now, but you can always count on me to bring everything back down. I got you for whatever ma." I felt like shit for being the cause of her falling out with her mother but damn, all I was doing was defending my chick.

"How do I know that everything you're saying is the truth? How do I know that you view me properly and just not as your property How do I know that you love me and just not lusting after me?"

"Where are all these questions coming from Butta?"

"All I'm trying to ask is how am I supposed to know that I made the right choice when you let some bitch that works for you disrespect me?"

"You trippin' about that shit with Camellia? I checked her ass when I felt she was being disrespectful."

"Yeah, you checked her, then her ass gonna call me Beamer."

"That shit wasn't even that serious Butta. You got shit coming at you from all these different places and you bugging out. Just chill ma."

"Can you just give me your keys, so I can leave please?"

"Can't do that. Get out the car." I stepped out and walked to the driver's side. I swung the door open and pulled her out.

"I was going to get out if you would've just gave me a second," she sassed.

"You weren't moving fast enough for me, I told her. I grabbed her hand and led her back up to the apartment.

"Well, look what Karma done dragged in," Camellia smirked as soon as we walked in the house."

"Camellia, why the fuck you testing me? The only time you need to be fuckin' talking is when you are apologizing to Royce."

181

"I don't need no apology from this bitch because she just mad I got something that she can no longer have. Can you just give me the keys to the house?"

"Oh bitch, you think you won a prize because you got Karma. You aren't the first one to have him and you damn sure won't be the last. You see, I was his first, which means I hold a special place in his heart that no bitch can ever take. From the way your face done hit the floor, I can tell he didn't tell you that. This nigga loved me and my pussy so much that he taught me how to cook up that work for him, just so he could have me near. So, about that apology; you might not want to wait on that because it's never going to happen."

"Camellia, you all the way out of-"

"No Karma, it's cool," Royce said, walking past me and over to Camellia. "Did you think you telling me you were Karma's first was going to make a difference to me because it doesn't. The person you getting right now really isn't me, but I feel a tad bit disrespected. Karma told me the only thing y'all got going on is business so that's how I see it. You don't have to say shit to me and I don't have to say shit to you. But what you won't do is try to throw dirt whenever you're in my presence. I'm a queen and should be treated as such. Now, I won't go as far as telling you that you need to bow whenever you see me but what I will say is that you need to not say shit when I'm around."

"Who the fuck do you think you are? Karma, you need to come get your-" were the only words Camellia was able to get out before Royce jumped on her ass. Royce was getting the best of her until Camellia ended up getting on top of Royce. Royce was still holding her own, but Camellia had the advantage. I snatched Camellia off of Royce and slung her behind me on the couch. I went to help Royce off the ground, but her little ass was already up and charging towards Camellia. I went and stepped in front of her, trying to stop her when her midget ass kicked me in my fucking dick.

Turning around, all I saw was Royce on top of Camellia, banging her head into the wall. I said fuck my dick pain and grabbed Royce up real fast before she killed this girl.

"Royce, chill the fuck out ma." Her chest was heaving up and done while tears streamed down her cheek. I didn't know what the fuck was going on with her, but I needed to get her out of here and I needed to check on Camellia because her ass wasn't moving.

"What the fuck happened in here?" Smitty asked, walking in the apartment.

"Just take Royce outside to the car please. While I check to make sure this girl is straight."

"Karma, if your ass ain't outside in two minutes, you can forget all about me," Royce cried as I passed her to Smitty.

"You could've gave her some tissue or something. She got snot and shit running down her nose man," Smitty complained.

"Shut the fuck up and just take her, damn," I barked.

"Ight, but you owe me."

I went over to where Camellia was to see if she was straight. Looking at her head, she had a gash but it wasn't deep or anything. I leaned down to see if she was still breathing when her lips connected to mine.

"Soft as hell, just like I remember," she smirked.

My hand wrapped around her neck tightly and firmly. "Don't you ever in your fuckin' life talk to Royce like that. She's just not just some regular bitch on the street; she's my bitch and you already know that I kill for mine. Was you my first pussy? Yeah, but you weren't my first love. Hell nah. That chick that just beat your ass, she's my first love and that trumps anything we ever fuckin' had. You dead ass walkin' on a thin line Camellia. Stop fucking playing around ight."

I let her ass go and left her there grasping for air. Going outside, I walked straight up to the car, telling Smitty I'd be back later. Getting in the car, I sped off while looking at Royce out the corner of my eye. She was sitting there with mixed emotions etched all on her face. Even though she was mad, she was still beautiful. It was like her beauty always found a way to shine through in the darkest of times.

"Wassup with you, Royce?" I asked. We were going to have this conversation because I was ready to get it over with. I'm sure she was upset about that shit Camellia said.

"I don't want to talk about it right now," she sighed.

"You might not want to talk about it, but this is something we have to talk about."

"I don't have to talk about anything if I don't want to; plus, there is nothing to say regardless. Camellia said everything that needed to be said."

"So, that's what you're mad about? You mad because of that shit Camellia said? Yeah, she was my first but you know that shit don't mean shit to me. The only thing that means something to me is you and the fact that you allowed Camellia to pull you out of character over some bullshit."

"What's bullshit to you isn't bullshit to me. You told me y'all just fucked, as if the two of you didn't have anything serious together."

"We did just fuck; nothing was serious between us on my end."

"She was your first Karma damn! Why don't you understand the significance of that? I'm sure she was the only one that you been fucking after all of these years. Tell me you had sex with other women while you been fucking her?"

She looked at me with tear stained cheeks; I pulled up in front of my house and cut off the ignition. I looked deep into her eyes, wondering if I should lie or tell the truth. Yeah, Camellia was the only bitch I was fucking because why would I fuck anything else when I had easy access to pussy? I tore my eyes away from hers, running my hand over my head.

"I'm going to keep it all the way honest because you deserve the truth. Camellia had been the only chick I been fucking, but there wasn't no feelings there."

"Yeah okay, Karma."

"Yeah okay Karma, nothing. I'm telling you what it is so believe that shit. I have no reason to lie to you because the truth would end up coming out sooner or later. If I didn't give a fuck about you, I would've lied to your face."

"I guess I should be saying thank you for telling me the truth, huh."

"I'm not trying to do this with you, Royce. Just tell me what's going to fix this shit."

"I can't tell you what's going to fix this because there is nothing to fix. As long as Camellia doesn't say nothing to me, then we cool; just make sure if you have to do business with her, you send Smitty or someone else. That bitch is foul and I don't want you around her ass. I'm sure if you give her a chance, that bitch would try to suck your dick in broad daylight," Royce sassed, getting out the car.

I got out behind her and jogged to catch up to her. I wrapped my arms around her waist, pulling her close to me. I inhaled her scent and nestled my face in the crook of her neck.

"You might as well stop because nothing is happening," she said while I unlocked the door.

"No one said something was gonna happen." I pushed her ass in the house, then closed the door behind us.

I walked right past Butta as if she wasn't even there. Walking in the room, I laid across the bed for a minute, trying to relieve all this stress. Between Trench and Camellia's bullshit, I didn't know how the fuck I was going to get shit back together. I was gonna have Trench handle Camellia since it seemed like he wanted to be boss like. It was crazy because I didn't even know who Trench was anymore. This nigga started switching up around the same time I met Royce. I wanted to ask Red his opinion on the situation, but he already wasn't feeling Trench and was telling me to watch him.

"What you doing in here staring up at the ceiling?" Royce asked, straddling me. My hands rested at her hips as I looked into her face.

"Nothing. You know you fucked Camellia up pretty good, right?" I didn't care that Royce fucked her up. I was just surprised her little ass could really throw them hands.

"Why do you care? Are you mad I hurt your little girlfriend?" She laughed.

"Hell nah, I'm not mad. As long as you straight, then I'm good and that's real shit. How you feeling though? You had a lot going on today."

"Karma, I don't even know how I should feel honestly. My mother and I have never gotten into an argument like the one we got into today. I wouldn't even say that we got into an argument, but the conversation we had was crazy. I never felt the need to defend my actions to my mother."

"A part of growing up is making your own decisions and doing what you feel is best. I know leaving your mother's house was hard for you because of the terms you left on. However, things will get better and I'm sure you will get right with your mother again;you just need to give it time."

"I know. I just don't understand why she would judge you over something that wasn't even that serious. You shot him in the dick; you didn't kill him."

"You see it that way but that doesn't mean your mother sees it that way. All your mom sees is a dude who carries guns around fucking her daughter. No mother wants their daughter to be with a nigga like me. I'm not the take home to mom type and I'm cool with that. People can judge me all they want, but I know my heart."

"I know your heart too, which is why I went so hard for you. For us. I believe in what we have."

"It's good that you believe in what we have because sometimes, I don't."

"You have doubts about us?" she questioned with a funny look on her face.

"I wouldn't say I have doubts but, for me, this shit is unrealistic."

"Why is it unrealistic?"

"Look at where I came from and look at where you came from. We from two different necks of the woods, yet you can still find it in your heart to love a nigga like me. I know I'm damaged goods but you still with a nigga. You supposed to be with a nigga working on wall street and shit like that. Royce, you not supposed to be with no thug like me."

Everything I was saying was exactly what I was feeling. To me, Royce was too good for me. She had a good head on her shoulders and she knew what she wanted out of life. The same things that attracted me to her were the same things I felt made me unworthy of her. I was a nigga without any parents who sold drugs to survive in this cold world.

"But who said you're a thug?"

"Shit, anyone who knows me would say I'm a thug. Stop acting like you don't what's up Butta."

"I'm not acting like I don't know what's up; just because the people in the streets label you a thug doesn't mean I'm going to. The way I see it, you're a survivor. You were left in this cold world alone. Instead of falling victim and just ending it all, you found a way out. Now, it may not be the most ideal way out but that doesn't take away from you making it.

When I look at you, all I see is Karma. I don't see the same Karma that you are in the streets. I see the Karma that's loving and would give me the world if I ask him to. I see the Karma that opened his heart to me. I see the Karma that reminded me of my worth and everything I deserve. The Karma I see isn't a thug; he is the man that I love and that I'm lucky to have." Her smile was infectious and I couldn't help but smile back at her. I placed my hand on the back of her head pulled her into my chest.

"I love you, Royce and you don't ever have to question that. You are the first and last girl to have my heart," I whispered.

"I love you too, Karma," she sobbed.

I laughed lightly because she was so damn emotional. I wiped her tears away from her eyes because there was no need for her to be crying. As far as I see it, it was us against the world. We stayed laid up until Smitty called me and said he needed me to come through. Shit, if I could, I would've stayed in this moment with Royce forever. It didn't feel like we were Royce and Karma; it felt like we were one. I know I sound like a straight bitch saying that shit, and honestly, I didn't give a fuck. Royce was everything I didn't think I deserved. She deserved to be showered with love and affection on a daily. She walked into my life and turned that shit upside down, but it was for the better. I wasn't saying that I was going to get married right now; all I'm saying is that Royce Silva was going to become Royce Montgomery in due time and that was my word.

Chapter 24: Royce

A week had gone by since I been staying with Karma and I honestly felt like shit. I never wanted to get out the bed and if I did, I would only be active for about two hours before I felt the need to get back in bed. I was constantly throwing up and never really wanted to eat anything. My emotions were at an all-time high and I was honestly becoming a bitch. I didn't know what the hell was wrong with me. At first, I thought it was because of everything that happened with my mother. I thought maybe the stress from that situation was causing me to become sick, even though I told myself that I didn't believe it.

Today was Thursday and it would be my first time working at The Cracked Mug. I was excited and nervous at the same time. I had been taking medicine all throughout the day, trying to help myself feel better because performing tonight was special to me.

"I'm just saying Royce; you need to take a pregnancy test. All you been doing is staying in the bed and throwing up," Callie complained.

I forgot she was even in the room with me talking because I been tuning her ass out since she got here. Karma didn't want me staying in the house alone, so he told me to call Callie over. That was the worst thing I could've ever done because she wouldn't shut up about me being pregnant.

"I wish you would shut up and let that go. I'm sick because I'm stressing, that's all. I know my body well enough that if I was pregnant, I would know," I told her.

"Say what you want but all the signs are there. You need to find out now before you end up too far along and no longer have options."

"What are you talking about options?" I asked her. I know she wasn't thinking what I think she was thinking because that wasn't even an option in my book.

"I'm talking about you getting an abortion." The way she said it made it seem as if it was nothing.

"You saying it like an abortion doesn't mean killing someone."

"Technically, it's not killing someone because the baby isn't even formed when the time comes to get an abortion."

"It doesn't matter Callie. Why would you even suggest I get an abortion?"

"I think you are taking this the wrong way."

"Then tell me how I should be taking it then," I snapped.

"All I'm saying is that you or Karma aren't ready to have any kids. I mean, look at Karma's background. He never had parents. so how is he supposed to raise a child?"

"Woah Callie, you are all the way out of bounds saying that shit," I told her, shocked.

"What it's the truth?"

"I told you that out of confidence, not for you to throw it back in my face. Regardless if Karma had parents or not, that will not affect the way he parents his own child. Callie, you got a lot of nerve talking about someone else's parents. Where the hell is your mom huh? The last time you heard from her, she was somewhere out hoeing. So, before you throw stones at Karma's house, make sure yours isn't made out of glass first."

"You think I give a fuck about you throwing my hoe of a mother in my face? Well, guess what bitch, I don't. I don't give a fuck about that bitch and I don't give a fuck about you. All I'm doing is trying to look out for you and be realistic. It's obvious that realistic is a little too much for you so let me tell you some lies to make you feel better. You and Karma will never be happy together because he's nothing but a fuck and you're nothing but a hopeless romantic.

You should've took your mother's advice and left his ass alone because he's not doing shit but cheating on your dumb ass. You thought you would've learned the signs from Addison. You will never be a wife because you don't know how to please a man. Ask me how I know Royce?" Callie yelled. My breathing picked up as I balled my fist and listened to my best friend throw insults at me, one after another.

"Royce, ask me how I know you can't please a man?"

193

"How?" I smirked slyly. This bitch just didn't know what was about to happen to her ass.

"Because after I rode Addison off into the heavens, the nigga started pillow talking. That's right, I fucked the shit out of Addison, then laughed when you would call his phone looking for him." Callie started laughing extremely hard.

Her laughter was silenced by my fist connecting with her face. I was raining blows on her as visions of her and Addison being together filled my head. The more the visions appeared, the angrier I got. I ended up dragging her by her hair down the stairs and towards the front door. She was kicking and screaming, but I honestly didn't give a fuck. She had disrespected me in more than one way within the last fifteen minutes.

Opening the front door, I dragged her ass on to the porch, then kicked the shit out of her. "I fucking hate you Callie. You ain't nothing but a hoe just like your rotten pussy mother. You should've been swallowed or flushed down the toilet; anything would've been better than you being born. Fucking stupid bitch!" I yelled, then slammed the front door.

Walking into the kitchen, I let out a gut wrenching scream while pulling my hair. I didn't want to believe that Callie had slept with Addison, but how could I not when she said it with so much conviction. The little fight I had with Callie had my body tired and worn out. As I was walking back up the stairs to go lay down before my show, I tripped over a box. Looking down, it was a pregnancy test. I picked it up and smirked because it must've fallen out of Callie's pocket when I dragged her ass.

Looking at the box had me feeling uneasy but, at the same time, it helped me to realize what I needed to do. I got so mad at Callie for telling me I should have an abortion when I wasn't even trying to take the test in the first place. Me not taking the test and finding out was me neglecting my possible child. Instead of going into the bed, I went into the bathroom and peed on the stick. The three minutes I waited was the longest minutes of my life. So many things went through my mind as I waited. Questions from I'm I going to be a good mother to is Karma gonna be there flashed through my mind.

When the time finally came for me to look at the test, I damn near passed out from looking at the results. I rushed into the bedroom, picking up the phone calling the only person I had left in this world.

"Wassup Butta, you straight? Are you gonna be able to sing tonight?" Karma answered the phone on the first ring and the sound of his voice made me nauseous. I dropped the phone and rushed to the bathroom to throw up before it hit the floor.

Chapter 25: Karma

"Royce!" I was calling out her name, but I wasn't getting any response. I was on my way to go talk to Red. He called me earlier and told me he wanted to see me asap. I didn't know what he wanted to talk to me about but it had to be important because he told me not to bring Trench. Even if I wanted to bring Trench, that shit would've been impossible. The nigga been on some straight solo dolo shit since that shit happened in the parking lot. Whenever I saw the nigga and tried to say wassup, he would be on some bitch shit and not acknowledge me. I wasn't pressed, so it didn't bother me. At the end of the day, as long as he was doing what needed to be done, I was cool.

I pulled over to the side, calling Royce again to make sure she was okay.

"Hello!"

"Yo, you ight? What happened to the phone?"

"I dropped it because I had to throw up."

"You need to go to the doctor because you still throwing up and shit. I don't care what you say but that's no stress."

"I know and that's why I'm calling you. We need to talk."

"Fuck," I said to myself. "Can us talking be put on hold? I need to go meet up with Red-"

"I understand that you're a boss who needs to handle business, but what we need to talk about is more important than anything else you have to do right now."

"Ight, but you gonna have to talk on the way over there," I told her.

"Whatever, just get here please," she sassed and hung up the phone.

Royce had been on some straight moody shit for the past week and that shit was irking my nerves. It was like she could never just chill. One minute, she would be good, and in a blink of an eye, she would be crying. I didn't understand the shit. I had to google the shit and the only thing I could come up with was that she was getting her period soon.

As I made a u-turn, I tried calling Red to let him know I was going to be a little late. His phone kept going to voicemail and straight off the back, I thought that shit was weird. In all the years I have known Red, his phone never went to voicemail. That shit was strange as fuck. I kept trying to call the whole way back to my house. When I pulled up, Royce was out front standing there with her arms crossed.

"Get in the car Butta."

"No, we are going to talk about this right here. Like I said, all that other shit you have to handle can wait."

"Royce, I'm not doing this with your emotional ass. Just get in the fucking car please."

Her stubborn ass got in the car and slammed her door hard as hell. I wanted to go off on her but didn't feel like starting an argument.

"What's up Butta? What you want to talk about?" I asked her, trying to get to the point. I had this strange ass feeling that something was wrong with Red.

"We are pregnant," she said, batting an eye.

"You what?" I questioned because I had to hear her wrong.

"I didn't say I was anything. I said we are pregnant," she repeated.

"How you know? You went to the doctor?"

"No, I didn't go to the doctor. I took a pregnancy test."

"You know them things are only ninety-nine point nine percent effective right."

"Really Karma! I can't fucking believe you. You really gonna tell me that there is a one percent chance that I'm not pregnant." In the middle of her rant, my phone started ringing. I looked down at the screen and it was Red calling.

Royce looked at the phone, then back at me with fire in her eyes. "If you answer that fucking phone, you might as well kiss me good bye."

"Butta, chill the fuck out ight," I told her and answered the phone.

"Yo Red, everything straight?" I asked while staring at Butta. She looked back at me with tears in her eyes. She leaned over, giving me a soft kiss on the lips before getting out the car. The kiss didn't feel like a regular kiss. It was more so a goodbye kiss. Butta could be in her feelings all she wanted but she would be ight later.

"Yo Red, you there my nigga?" I asked when I realized I hadn't gotten a response.

"Tr... Tre..." I could hear Red's voice, but it was faint as hell.

"Red! Red" I yelled into the phone.

"Tre... Tren..." he said again before there was no longer any breathing.

I quickly hung up the phone, then called Red's number back. It went straight to voicemail. I called and called again but kept getting the same outcome. The next person I called was Max, but his shit went right to voicemail too. I looked towards the house thinking about running after Royce, but I had to find out what was up with Red.

Before pulling off, I sent Royce a text, letting her know that I loved her and we would finish talking once I handled this. I sped through the streets on a mission to get to Red's office in half the time it took. When I got to his office, I didn't even turn the ignition off. I put the car in park, then jumped out, heading inside. It was quiet as fuck, which was odd; his body guards and Max were usually always around. I pulled my gun out ready for whatever. If I was going to die here, then I would be ight because the last thing I told Royce was I love her. Red's office door was open wide.

I didn't even bother walking in because it would've been a waste of time. I left out the building and jumped in my car. While pulling off, I dialed 911.

"911, what is your emergency?"

"I heard gun shots over on a hundred and twenty fifth, at the old pool hall."

"Okay Sir, are you-" I hung up the phone, doing eighty in a fifty-five zone.

A nigga was all fucked up on the inside. The only fucking parent figure I had ever known was dead because of some nigga that wanted to be a boss. One of our own had went against the grain because of greed. I now understood what Red was trying to say on the phone before it went blank.

"Ayo Smitty, where Trench at?" I asked him as soon as he answered the phone.

"I don't know; the nigga been gone for a minute."

"How long exactly has he been gone?" I questioned.

"I don't know, maybe like two hours or something. This nigga just walked in the door; you want me to put him on the phone."

"Nah, you good. I'm on my way over there; just make sure that nigga don't go no fucking where."

"Ight, I got you," Smitty said, hanging up the call.

My heart was in pain and the only thing on my mind was revenge. As if Royce knew I was busy, she started ringing my phone down. Without thinking, I took my phone and threw the shit out the window. I couldn't deal with her shit right now because I had more important shit to worry about. Red was fucking dead and, at this moment, that's the only thing that fucking mattered. Red was the last thing I had on this earth and now he was gone. Niggas didn't know, but they had just released the beast.

Chapter 26: Smitty

"Aye, hold shit down for me right quick. I'm about to have Callie suck me off right quick. You want me to bring her over here so you can see what you been missing." I laughed, staring at Trench.

"You talk a lot of shit for a dead nigga walking," he smirked.

"The fuck is you saying?" I asked him.

"You already know what it is. There's a time and place for everything, remember that shit," Trench said.

I waved that nigga off because he wasn't really about shit. Trench was one of those dudes that loved to talk shit without putting any action behind his words. The nigga done told me I was gonna die so many times that I found the shit hilarious. The only reason why I would say anything back was to see him bitch up when it came to put his money where his mouth was.

Uncle died on the spot, pop killed the family with heroine shots. Gave my life to the block. Figured I get shot least I die on top. I came alive in the drop. Big body all white shit looked like a yacht. I got a five grand a pop. I had a plug in Saint Thomas on trillion watts. Flew him back to the states park 92 bricks in front of five 60 state. Now the Nets don't throw from where I used to throw bricks, so it's only right I'm still tossing 'round Knicks, uh."

Jay Z's verse from that song *Seen it all* came blaring through my phone. Looking down at my screen, a nigga was tempted on sending the bitch to voicemail. Stepping out the door and into the hallway, I went against my better judgment and answered the phone anyway.

"What you want?" I questioned.

"I been calling your phone for days; why are you acting like you don't see my phone calls?" she whined into the phone.

"Give me a good reason on why I should answer your phone calls. In all the years we been together, I have only asked you to do one fucking thing and yo raggedy ass couldn't even do that."

"How is it my fault that Karma wouldn't open up to me?"

"How isn't it your fault? A bitch came around and made this nigga fall in love in two fucking months. She did something that you couldn't do in five years."

"That's not fair Smitty," she cried.

"Camellia, stop with all that crying shit. You should already know tears don't effect me."

"I'm sorry Smitty; I have tried my best. I swear I have tried my best. Just because I couldn't do what you needed me to do means you go and cheat on me with Callie!" she yelled.

"I'm not cheating on you with Callie. I'm simply getting her to do what the fuck you weren't capable off. Matter of fact, lose my fucking number because yo ass is useless to me now." I hung up the phone, not even bothering to let her get a word in.

"What you doing outside the door?" Karma asked, scaring the fuck out of me.

"Nothing, I was on the phone talking to Callie and shit. She was straight bugging. You know that nigga in there still caught up on her, so I didn't want him hearing me say her name."

Karma nodded his head, then walked right past me and into the house. I followed him in because something seemed off about him. The nigga seemed cold as fuck, like he just lost his soul or something. On some real shit, I could've sworn I felt a chill when he walked passed me.

"Trench, get the fuck up my nigga," he said.

"Who the fuck you talkin' to?" Trench asked, standing up and grilling Karma.

"Nigga, I'm fucking talkin' to you." Karma pulled out two of his guns, pointing them both at Trench.

"Nigga, you not the only one with…." Trench was never able to finish his words because Karma started firing shots. He emptied one clip then dropped the gun, walking towards Trench's bullet filled body. He stood over him, looking down at him with no mercy in his eyes. Aiming at his head, he emptied his second gun into Trench's head. Skull, brain matter, and blood splattered all over Karma and the nigga didn't even flinch once.

"Clean this shit up, then meet me at my crib," he said, walking past me and out the door.

When I heard the door close, a grin spread across my face. These niggas were dumber than I fucking thought. Pulling out my phone, I scrolled my call log looking for a certain number. Once I found it, I pressed dial and waited for the person to pick up the phone.

"You better be calling me with good news!" the person on the line said.

"Lose all that fucking bass in your voice because you work for me and not the other way around. Shit is on the up and up. Karma just came in here and laid Trench the fuck out. No questions asked."

"That's good, now we can move to phase two of our plan."

"Nigga, you don't have to fucking tell me we can move on. Don't forget, it's my fucking plan."

"Nah nigga, don't you forget that it was me that opened your fucking eyes to this shit."

"Yeah, whatever nigga. Just remember at the end of this shit, I'm gonna be the head nigga in charge. Respect my gangsta or get laid the fuck down," I spat, then hung up.

Looking at Trench's dead body, I shook my head. "Charge it to the game." I laughed.

Shit was about to get real in these streets and I couldn't fucking wait. Karma wasn't gonna know what the fuck hit him because he was too caught up in that bitch Royce. While this nigga was busy falling in love, I was busy putting moves into motion to be crowned the king. It was my time to shine and nobody couldn't tell me shit. Smitty was about to be the name people feared in these streets. Shit, just like I said on the phone, niggas could either respect my gangsta or get laid the fucked down. Either way, I planned to be the last one standing.

To Be Continued………..

CPSIA information can be obtained
at www.ICGtesting.com
Printed in the USA
LVOW12s1748310816

502664LV00003B/603/P